Mr Darcy's Rescue

Darcy and Elizabeth What If? #2

JENNIFER LANG

© Jennifer Lang 2014
The moral right of the author has been asserted

No part of this publication may be reproduced, stored in a retrieval system, or transmitted in any form or by any means without the prior permission in writing of the publisher. Nor be otherwise circulated in any form of binding or cover other than that in which it is published and without a similar condition including this condition being imposed on the subsequent purchaser.
This book is a work of fiction. The characters and incidents are either fictitious or are used fictitiously. Any resemblance to any real person or incident is entirely coincidental and not intended by the author.

Also by Jennifer Lang

The Darcy and Elizabeth What If? Series

These novellas are all separate, standalone stories. They can be read in any order.

#1 Elizabeth's Mistake

Chapter One

Elizabeth Bennet was in the garden on a bright sunny morning, cutting roses for the house. It was a gentleman's residence made of golden stone and the garden was in full bloom, sending sweet perfume into the air. When her basket was full she put her scissors on top of the basket and then, her light muslin gown fluttering around her ankles , she went back inside. She took the flowers into the flower room and arranged them in a porcelain vase, which she set on the table in the hall, and then she noticed that the post had arrived. She looked at the letters as she took them into the drawing-room and handed the most interesting one to her mother.

'Oh, it is a letter from your aunt Gardiner, I wonder what she has to say?' said Mrs Bennet.

Jane looked up. She was sitting on one of the elegant sofas, embroidering a handkerchief.

'How is my aunt?' asked Elizabeth as her mother unfolded the letter.

'She is very well,' said Mrs Bennet. 'How could she be otherwise? Your aunt does not have my worries. She does not have five daughters all out, and not one of them married. When your father dies, we will all be turned out of the house! Jane, at least, tried to catch a husband the last time she was in London' – this was a wholly distorted view of the truth, for Jane had never "tried to catch a husband" in her life – 'but you, Lizzy, seem to make no effort at all. Ah!' Her face rose and she looked up with a smile. 'Here is a chance for you! Your aunt and uncle are going to Ramsgate soon as your uncle has not been well recently. His physician says the sea air will do him good, and as Ramsgate is not too far from London, that is the place that has been chosen. Your aunt writes that she will give you both a holiday. She will take you first, Lizzy, for two weeks, and then Jane for the next two.'

'I wish I was going to Ramsgate!' said Lydia, coming into the room with a heavy sigh. 'I never go anywhere. La! Life is so boring.'

'We will persuade your aunt to take you next time,' said Mrs Bennet. 'Now, Lizzy, you must have a new dress and a new bonnet. There will be plenty of eligible gentlemen in Ramsgate and I am sure you will be engaged by the time you come home. And Jane, you must have something new, too. There will be plenty of young men in Ramsgate for both of you.'

'My aunt should have invited me. I know I would come home with a husband, if I could only go!' said Lydia, throwing herself down on the sofa.

'Yes, my love, I am sure you would,' said her doting mother. 'You are always very clever where the gentlemen are concerned.'

Elizabeth and Jane exchanged exasperated

glances, but they knew it was no use saying anything. Their mother had always been partial to Lydia and encouraged her in her waywardness.

'I am grateful to my aunt for thinking of me,' said Lizzy. 'The summer is very hot and some sea bathing will be wonderful. I only wish we were going together,' she said, turning to Jane, 'but I dare say there would not be room for both of us at the same time.'

'I would like some sea bathing, too,' said Lydia. 'I would like to trundle into the waves in a bathing machine. La! What fun! I would bathe in my petticoat and I am sure I would look very fetching in the water.'

'Yes, Lydia, I am sure you would,' agreed her mother.

'When am I to go?' asked Elizabeth.

Her mother continued reading the letter, then said, 'You are to go next week. You will stay with your aunt and uncle in Gracechurch Street for a night before you travel on to Ramsgate with them. You must make yourself useful, for I am sure your aunt will need help with the children, but do not neglect your appearance. If you are not married by the end of the summer I will despair of you altogether. And Jane, I am sure you will do your best, too. You cannot be so beautiful for nothing. But a woman's bloom soon fades, you know, and you are two-and-twenty already, so you must make the most of every opportunity that comes your way.'

'I am sure I will be married long before I am two-and-twenty,' said Lydia. 'Why, Jane is practically an old maid.'

Elizabeth suppressed a smile, for anyone less like an old maid than Jane would be hard to imagine. Jane combined a serene temperament with a beautiful face, and Lizzy felt that any man would be very lucky to win her affections.

'I had better go into Meryton and tell your aunt Philips the news,' said Mrs Bennet.

'I will come with you,' said Lydia, jumping up. 'I want to see if there are any new bonnets in the milliner's.'

'Of course, my dear Lydia, I am always glad of your company. Your aunt is always pleased to see you, too.'

Mrs Bennet and Lydia went to get ready, while Elizabeth and Jane went back into the garden to finish cutting the roses.

'Mama did not express herself very well, but it is true that we will have a chance to make some new acquaintances in Ramsgate,' said Jane. 'The only pity is that we will not be there together. But I dare say that would make it too much of a crush.'

'Yes, there will be a full house with my aunt, uncle and the children, as well as the servants. But in a way it will be better like this, because we will be able to write to each other and share all the news,' said Lizzy.

'Oh, yes! You must write to me every day and tell me what you are doing.'

'I will,' Elizabeth promised her. 'And you must write to me and tell me all the news from home.'

The following week, Elizabeth set out. Her sisters accompanied her to the local coaching inn, where she boarded the stagecoach for London. One of the Longbourn maids went with her, to protect her reputation and add to her consequence.

Elizabeth had a happy temperament and she enjoyed the journey. The scenery was varied. The coach rolled through pretty country lanes and quaint market towns, and it ran alongside streams and over rivers. The sun shone down on green fields and stone cottages, with venerable old trees casting dappled shade over the landscape.

At last the coach neared London. There was much more bustle and noise than there had been in the country. As they went into the capital, the carriages became more numerous and the jingling of harness mingled with the clopping of horses' hooves. There were shouts from the pie men who walked along with trays of pies carried on their heads, and people selling fruit shouted out, 'Come and try!' There were nursemaids with children, and all manner of other people going about their business.

The coach turned into the yard of the coaching inn and the carriage drew to a halt. As Elizabeth climbed out of the coach, she saw that her uncle's carriage was waiting for her. She climbed into its comfortable interior and before long she had been transported to her aunt and uncle's house in Gracechurch Street.

There was a warm welcome waiting for her. Mrs Gardiner was a sensible woman and Elizabeth loved her very much. Mr Gardiner, too, was a sensible man and Elizabeth was sorry to see him looking pale. But she knew that some sea air would put colour in his cheeks.

The children ran to greet Elizabeth and she gave them the presents she had brought from Longbourn. It was a happy, lively meeting.

Elizabeth went upstairs, to the room she always had when staying with her aunt. She washed and made herself tidy and then went downstairs for dinner.

There was plenty of news to catch up with and the evening passed quickly. But, despite her busy day, Elizabeth found it hard to sleep. She was excited about going to Ramsgate, for she did not often have a chance to go to the seaside. Her father was not fond of travelling and so her summers were usually spent at Longbourn.

But morning came at last. They made a good breakfast – all except her uncle, who had little appetite – and then everything was put into the carriage. Most of the servants had already gone down to Ramsgate, but the few who remained made sure everything was packed properly and then they were off – all except a footman and a maid, who were left behind to look after the house.

The journey was much more lively than Elizabeth's journey of the day before. The children were excited and, although well behaved, they chattered and fidgeted, so that the adults were glad when at last they arrived.

As Elizabeth stepped out of the coach, her senses revelled in the newness of it all: the tang of salt on her lips, the cry of the gulls overhead, the expanse of blue ocean stretching out in front of her – so different to the green fields at home – and the smell of the fresh sea air. She breathed in deeply and felt fortunate to be there.

Her young cousins climbed out of the coach. They had been cramped for hours and they ran across the pavement and skipped up the steps to the town house, using up some of their energy.

'Oh, what a relief,' said Mrs Gardiner, as she looked up at the house.

Elizabeth understood her at once. The Gardiners had not been to Ramsgate before and so they had taken the house on a recommendation from a friend. Mrs Gardiner had been anxious, not knowing what to expect, but fortunately the house was attractive and well kept. It was in a row of similar houses and it was painted pink. Well-polished windows with small panes were set in white frames. The windows were open and the curtains were blowing gently in the breeze. The houses further along the row were painted in a variety of different colours, adding to the novelty and cheerfulness of the scene.

They went up a short flight of stone steps to the front door, which was painted white to match the windows, and was set with a brass knocker.

The door opened as if by magic and Mrs Gardiner's housekeeper welcomed them.

The children ran through the spacious hall and up the stairs. Mrs Gardiner was attending to her husband and so Elizabeth guided the children to the top floor, where their rooms were to be found. She left them with their nurse and then followed the housekeeper to the floor below.

'Your room is here, miss,' said the housekeeper.

It was a large apartment with a tall window overlooking the sea. The sky was a bright blue and the sun was shining. The weather had encouraged people to walk along the seafront, and Elizabeth amused herself by studying them, for she was a student of human nature.

There were several families with young children, accompanied by nurses. Some of the nurses were pushing perambulators. Others were holding young children by the hand, or keeping an eye on older, more adventurous children.

There were a number of couples. The ladies had colourful parasols and their muslin skirts fluttered in the breeze. The gentlemen wore blue coats and cream pantaloons, and they doffed their hats as they greeted acquaintances.

And there, at the end of the promenade, was a young lady with a companion. The young lady was hardly more than a girl, perhaps about fifteen years of age. She was very well dressed and she had an air of consequence about her. Behind her walked a footman.

Elizabeth wondered who she was. But she did not have time to wonder for long. The gong sounded and she hurriedly tidied herself and then went downstairs.

Her aunt and uncle were already seated in the drawing-room and her aunt was presiding over the teapot.

Her uncle looked even paler than he had done the previous day and Elizabeth was glad he had decided to take some time away from his business so he could recover his health. His physician could find nothing actually wrong with him and said that he had simply been overworking.

'I think we will be very happy here,' said Aunt Gardiner.

Elizabeth agreed.

After tea, she said, 'I would like to walk

along the promenade. After spending all day in the coach I would appreciate some exercise.'

'You will excuse me, I am sure,' said Mrs Gardiner. 'I want to see that everything is unpacked. Your uncle, too, I fear is tired.'

'Yes, I am,' he admitted.

Elizabeth knew her duty, and besides, it would be a pleasure to help her aunt, so she said, 'Then I will stay and help you.'

'There is no need for that. I know how much you love to walk, Lizzy. Tomorrow I will come with you, but for today, make sure you take the maid. It will not do to walk about Ramsgate on your own. We are not in the country now.'

Elizabeth agreed. At home, she did not need to take a chaperone every time she ventured out of the house, but the rules of behaviour were stricter in public places.

'There are one or two commissions you can do for me while you are out,' said her aunt. 'I have forgotten to bring any white thread and I am sure to need it. And I have forgotten my fine needles.'

Elizabeth put on her shawl and her bonnet, and then set out with the maid. She almost skipped down the front steps, so glad was she to be out of doors, and she made her way down to the sea. The tide was coming in and the waves were fringed with white as they broke with a swooshing sound against the sandy beach.

She breathed in deeply as she walked along

the promenade and into the town. Coming towards her was the young lady she had seen from her window. The young lady was very finely dressed indeed, but it was her sweet expression which drew Elizabeth's interest. The young lady seemed to be alone, apart from her servants, and Elizabeth wondered if the young lady's family were not in town.

A sudden gust of wind caught Elizabeth's bonnet and she put her hand on her head to hold it in place.

The young lady did likewise, but she was not so fortunate. The ribbon tying her bonnet beneath her chin came loose, and the wind tore the bonnet from her head, sending it tumbling and dancing towards Elizabeth.

Elizabeth reached out and caught it as it flew past.

'Oh, thank you!' said the young lady, as she approached with a blush. 'I thought I had lost it and I would be very sorry to do that. It was a present from my brother. May I do anything to help you in return?'

Elizabeth said, 'Yes, I believe you may. I am looking for the haberdasher's. I have to buy some needles and thread for my aunt. I am new here and so I do not yet know my way about.'

The young lady retrieved her bonnet from Elizabeth, but when she examined it she let out an exclamation of dismay.

'Oh!' she said, 'The ribbon has blown away.'

It was true, the ribbon was missing. Elizabeth looked up and saw it spiralling ever higher in the sky as the wind took it and blew it out to sea.

'I will have to buy some more,' said the young lady. 'We could walk to the haberdasher's together, if you wish. It will be easier for me to show you the way than to explain.'

Elizabeth thanked her and they set off together.

'Have you been here long?' asked Elizabeth.

'I have been here for several weeks,' the young lady said. 'It was very hot in London and my brother felt I should be happier by the sea.'

'He seems very attentive. You are lucky to have someone who cares for you so dearly.'

'Yes, I am. Do you have any brothers?'

'No,' said Elizabeth.

'Oh, I am sorry,' said the young lady. 'I do not know what I would do without mine. He has looked after me ever since our parents died.'

Elizabeth said how sorry she was to hear the young lady was an orphan, but the young lady disclaimed it, saying she was very fortunate in so many ways that she was not to be pitied.

'I do have four sisters, though,' said Elizabeth.

'Four! I am sure I envy you. I have always wanted a sister, someone to talk to and share things with. My brother is very dear to me but I do not want to bore him too much with talk of bonnets!'

Elizabeth said, 'I have a sister of about your age who never thinks of anything else!'

The young lady smiled. 'I am sure I hope I think of other things besides, but it is very pleasant to talk of clothes, all the same. But forgive me, I have not introduced myself. I am not yet out, you see, and I do not always know the right way of doing things, so I hope you will excuse me if I make a mistake and do not do everything just as I should. I am Miss Darcy, and this is my companion, Mrs Younge.'

'And I am Miss Elizabeth Bennet. I am staying in Ramsgate with my aunt and uncle, Mr and Mrs Gardiner.'

'I hope we might see something of each other while you are here,' ventured Miss Darcy. 'Would you care to come to tea tomorrow afternoon?'

'I should like it very much,' said Elizabeth.

Miss Darcy gave her the address and the two ladies went into the haberdasher's, feeling very pleased with each other. Although Miss Darcy was four or five years younger than Elizabeth, she was still old enough to be a friend and companion. Elizabeth was glad to have made a friend in Ramsgate and she knew that Miss Darcy felt the same.

Elizabeth bought the needles and thread for her aunt while Miss Darcy examined a selection of ribbon.

'I cannot decide,' said Miss Darcy.

'This one is very nice,' said Mrs Younge.

Elizabeth was surprised at the companion. The ribbon was scarlet and totally unsuitable for such a young lady. It would also not match her complexion.

'I think this one would be better,' said Elizabeth, picking up a pale green ribbon which would be more suitable for Miss Darcy's tender years. It would also match her eyes.

'Oh, yes, it's very pretty,' said Miss Darcy. She said to the shopkeeper, 'I will have a yard and a half of that one, please.'

Elizabeth was just about to bid her new friend goodbye when the door opened and a very handsome gentleman entered the shop. He was of medium height with fair hair and a good figure. He was dressed in a blue tailcoat and cream breeches with black shoes. He took off his hat and tucked it under his arm. Then, ignoring Elizabeth completely, he went over to her new friend, smiling all the while.

'Why, if it isn't Miss Darcy again! What a pleasant surprise!' he said, his eyes twinkling attractively.

He bowed and kissed Miss Darcy's hand.

Miss Darcy blushed.

'We do seem to keep meeting, Mr Wickham,' she said.

'We do indeed! But in such a small town, it is difficult not to,' he said. 'I cannot be sorry for it, in fact I am very glad of it. We are such old friends that it is always a pleasure to see you and I welcome this chance to renew our acquaintance.'

Miss Darcy turned to Elizabeth and said, 'This is Mr Wickham. He is —'

'A family friend,' interrupted Mr Wickham smoothly. 'We grew up together on the same estate. Miss Darcy's brother and I are friends.'

'Oh! I am so pleased you are friends again,' said Miss Darcy, turning to him with a smile. 'I did not like it when he was angry with you. It is so much pleasanter when everyone gets along together.'

'Our disagreement was nothing. It was just the usual falling out between friends, the sort of thing that blows over in a few weeks,' said Mr Wickham with a charming smile. 'We are now even better friends than ever. I see you have been buying ribbon. A very pretty choice, if I may say so. And now, if you have finished here, perhaps you would allow me to escort you home?'

Miss Darcy looked at her companion, who said, 'There can be no objection to it I am sure.'

The shopkeeper wrapped her ribbon, then she picked up her parcel and took Mr Wickham's arm. She bid Elizabeth goodbye and the two of them left the shop, followed by the companion.

Elizabeth was left looking after them, feeling uneasy. Mr Wickham was handsome and charming but he reminded her of the fox in the fairy story about the gingerbread man. The fox was wily and cunning and told the gingerbread man he would carry him across the river on his nose. But when the gingerbread man trusted him, and the fox carried him far out over the water, the fox gobbled him up.

Elizabeth could not help feeling that Mr Wickham intended to gobble Miss Darcy up. He had quickly smoothed over any suggestion that Miss Darcy's brother did not like him, and he had cut Miss Darcy off when she was about to tell Elizabeth about him. He had been altogether too glib and she found she did not trust George Wickham.

Even worse, she did not trust Miss Darcy's companion.

A look had passed between these two when Mr Wickham had first entered the shop, and Elizabeth found herself with grave misgivings. Miss Darcy was evidently an heiress. She was in Ramsgate alone apart from servants. And although her brother was obviously very caring, he was not here to watch over her.

As Elizabeth walked back along the seafront, she wondered what she should do.

She decided she must talk it over with her Aunt Gardiner and see if she was justified in saying something to Miss Darcy. The two young ladies were only slightly acquainted after all, and Miss Darcy might view it as an impertinence.

Elizabeth put it out of her mind for the rest of her walk. The fresh breeze was enlivening. The sight of the fishing boats bobbing on the water, together with the fishermen mending their nets on the beach, had all the interest of novelty and she took a keen interest in everything she saw.

When she returned to the house she recognised it easily, despite its being the same style as all the others in the row, because of its cheerful pink colour.

As she went inside she saw there were boxes everywhere, but most of them were now empty. The servants had been busy unpacking and the house was taking on a more homely air.

Elizabeth removed her outdoor clothes and then went into the drawing-room. She found her aunt there, alone.

'How is my uncle?' asked Elizabeth.

'Tired,' said Mrs Gardiner. 'I have sent him to bed.'

'And the children?'

'They are in the garden. It is not very large, but their governess felt they needed some fresh air and I agreed. It was a long journey but they behaved very well. Tomorrow I have promised we will take them down to the beach.'

'Oh, yes, that will be fun,' said Elizabeth. 'Will we be going in the morning? I only ask because I have been invited out to tea tomorrow afternoon.'

'Oh? Really? Well in that case, yes, we will go to the beach in the morning. But where are you going? Who has invited you? How did it come about?'

Mrs Gardiner was very interested in everything Elizabeth had to tell her. She smiled when Elizabeth spoke of Miss Darcy but then frowned when Elizabeth told her about Mr Wickham.

'What do you think I should do?' asked Elizabeth, when she had told her aunt everything. 'Do you think I am justified in saying anything to Miss Darcy?'

Mrs Gardiner thought for a few minutes.

'Yes, I think you are,' she said at last. 'You cannot say too much to begin with, but I think you should certainly give her a hint – just enough to put her on her guard. And then, when you come to know her better, you will be able to say more.'

Elizabeth agreed.

Her aunt was very quiet.

'What is it?' asked Elizabeth.

'Oh, nothing. I was just wondering if your new friend could have a connection to the Pemberley Darcys. I used to live in Derbyshire, as you know, and the greatest family in the neighbourhood was named Darcy. I believe they had a daughter and I have been trying to recall her name. I left the neighbourhood before she was born, and I have only heard of her through friends. But I think – yes, I think her name was Georgiana. If it is the same family, then she is a very great heiress indeed. I knew her father a little. He was very wealthy, but above that, he was a very good man and he was well liked in the neighbourhood.'

'I will ask her tomorrow if it is the same family,' said Elizabeth.

'Yes, do. And, once your uncle is feeling better, we must invite her to tea. And now, I had better go and see the housekeeper. She has done very well but there are one or two things I want changing.'

Her aunt left the room.

Elizabeth took the opportunity of writing to Jane. She went over to the small rosewood writing table in the corner, where she sat down on the matching rosewood chair, sweeping the skirt of her muslin gown beneath her. She took up a quill and dipped it in the ink. She took a few minutes to order her thoughts and then she began. There was already a lot to tell her sister, and she filled three pages with news before she was done.

The following day, Elizabeth spent an invigorating morning on the beach with her family. Her aunt and uncle sat on a bench in the warm sunshine, while Elizabeth played with the children. They all had kites and she helped the children to fly them, running along the beach until the kites were caught by the wind and flew into the air.

There were a few tears as some of the kites refused to fly, or became tangled, but at last every kite was made to soar aloft and the children's laughter could be heard mingling with the swoosh of the waves and the cry of the gulls.

It was a happy party that returned to the house for luncheon. The sea air had given Mr Gardiner an appetite and he ate more than usual, which encouraged Mrs Gardiner. The wind and the sun had put some colour in his cheeks, and although he retired to his room after lunch, Elizabeth and her aunt were pleased to see the holiday appeared to be doing him some good.

Elizabeth's aunt took out her sewing basket.

'Thank you for these needles, they are just what I need,' said her aunt.

Elizabeth joined her aunt in her sewing until it was time for her to leave.

'Now, Lizzy, you must be off,' said Mrs Gardiner. 'It will not do to keep Miss Darcy waiting. You must take the maid. I will not let anyone say that we do not look after you!'

Elizabeth kissed her aunt on the cheek. Then, putting on her pelisse, gloves and bonnet, she picked up her reticule and set out, accompanied by the maid. After a brisk walk along the seafront she arrived at an imposing residence which was twice the size of that taken by her aunt and uncle. She was admitted by a footman, who led her through to the drawing-room, where he announced her.

Miss Darcy was sitting at the pianoforte. She jumped up as soon as Elizabeth was announced.

'How glad I am to see you!' she said, coming forward with hands outstretched.

Elizabeth took her hands and the two women exchanged greetings.

Mrs Younge did not look so pleased to see Elizabeth.

'Let me help you with your bonnet,' said Miss Darcy.

It was evident she was enjoying her chance to be a hostess.

Elizabeth thanked her and she was soon sitting on the sofa as one of the servants whisked her bonnet and pelisse away.

Then Miss Darcy turned to her companion.

'Mrs Younge, would you fetch my book of engravings. I left it in my room and I would like to show it to Miss Bennet.'

Mrs Younge did not look as though she liked to leave the two of them alone together, but she could not refuse and so she left the room.

'My aunt was very interested to hear your name,' said Elizabeth. 'She used to live in Derbyshire and wondered if you could be related to the Darcys of Pemberley?'

Miss Darcy gave an attractive, light laugh.

'Why, that is who I am. Miss Darcy of Pemberley! What a small world it is.'

'Yes, indeed,' said Elizabeth.

They fell into easy conversation. It was not long before Miss Darcy invited Elizabeth to call her Georgiana.

'Miss Darcy and Miss Bennet sound so formal!' she said. Adding with a blush, 'And I am sure we are going to be friends.'

'So am I,' said Elizabeth warmly.

She invited Georgiana to call her Elizabeth and the two of them entered into a delightful conversation about their hobbies and interests.

At last, Elizabeth was able to say, casually, 'Your brother must be pleased to learn that Mr Wickham is here, if the two of them are such good friends.'

'I do not believe my brother knows about it. At least, he did not mention it in his last letter,' said Georgiana.

'Then you must tell him,' said Elizabeth. 'I am sure he will want to know.'

'I thought so, too, but Mrs Younge said there was no need to tell him.'

'You know your brother better than Mrs Younge does,' said Elizabeth. 'If you think he will like to know, then I am sure he will.'

'I am so glad to have you here! You give me confidence. Mrs Younge says things sometimes . . . I am not sure she really knows as much as she thinks she does. She has not been in society for some time – she is a widow, you know – and I think her advice is not always good. I have sometimes wondered about it before, but because I never had anyone to ask, I followed her advice. But now I will do as you say. I have already written to my brother this week but I will mention it in my next week's letter. It might even encourage Fitzwilliam to visit me.'

She spoke a little wistfully.

Elizabeth said, 'Does he not come here very often?'

'Oh, yes! He has visited me several times already. But he has a great deal of business to attend to, you know. Pemberley is a large estate and there are a lot of decisions to be made. He has not been for some weeks, however, and I would like to see him again. You will like him, I am sure,' she said artlessly. She went over to her writing table and picked up a letter. 'Does he not write well?' she said, showing the letter to Elizabeth.

Elizabeth smiled at Georgiana's attractive love for her brother. It matched her own love for her sister, Jane. But a brother was not a sister, and Elizabeth could see why Georgiana should be in need of female company of her own age.

Elizabeth looked at the letter. It was written in a strong, flowing hand. Its style was very formal and full of long words, but even so, Mr Darcy's love for his sister shone through.

Elizabeth handed the letter back to

Georgiana.

'He writes very well indeed,' she said.

Georgiana looked pleased and put the letter back on her desk.

Mrs Younge returned with the book of engravings and the young ladies examined it until tea was brought in.

Tea was a very grand affair. The tea itself was in a silver tea pot, with a silver milk jug and silver sugar bowl. These three items were set on a silver tray, which also contained china cups and saucers, as well as china plates. A selection of small sandwiches, scones and cakes were served on a china cake stand.

Georgiana poured the tea into the delicate cups, moving a little self consciously as she was clearly not used to doing it, but she acquitted herself as a hostess very well.

After tea, the two young ladies looked through a book of fashion plates and discussed the latest styles, before it was time for Elizabeth to depart. But she did not do so before they had decided to meet on the promenade the following morning, when they would walk together and continue their friendship.

The writer of the proudly displayed letter, Mr Fitzwilliam Darcy, was sitting in the dining-room of Darcy House almost two weeks later, partaking of a breakfast of steak and eggs. He had spent most of the summer at his London house but he was ready for a change. He would go and see his sister in Ramsgate again at the end of the week.

He was half way through his breakfast when the post was brought in. The footman, as usual, put the letters on a silver salver on the sideboard.

Once Mr Darcy had finished his breakfast, the footman carried the salver over to the table.

Mr Darcy leafed through the letters and then stopped when he came to one addressed in his sister's handwriting. It had gone first of all to Pemberley, where he would have been if business had not detained him in town, but the staff at Pemberley were very efficient and they had sent it on to London. He smiled and opened it, reading it with pleasure. But then his brow furrowed. It seemed his sister had made a friend in Ramsgate, a Miss Elizabeth Bennet.

Bennet. Bennet, he thought. He did not know the name and he doubted if Miss Bennet would be a suitable friend for Miss Darcy of Pemberley. However, it could do no very great harm, he supposed, especially as it seemed that Miss Bennet was shortly to return to London.

But then he read something that concerned him more. George Wickham was in Ramsgate. He read his sister's letter with growing alarm.

I am so pleased to learn that you and George are no longer enemies. He told me all about it, how it was nothing but a silly quarrel between you, and how you are now friends. He has been calling on me nearly every day and I have been glad to see him. He is a reminder of Pemberley . . .

Mr Darcy stood up in a hurry, pushing his chair back so quickly the legs scraped against the floor.

'Have the carriage brought round to the front of the house at once,' he said.

The footman bowed and went to carry out his order.

Mr Darcy went upstairs and told his valet to pack a bag.

Less than an hour later, he was on his way to Ramsgate.

Chapter Two

Elizabeth, too, received a letter that morning, but its contents were not nearly so alarming. The letter was from her sister, Jane, and contained all the news from home.

I must confess I am looking forward to my holiday. Mama's nerves have been troublesome, and Lydia has been more than usually vexing. She is bored, and says so at every opportunity. Kitty is fractious and Mary is even more moralising than usual. It is the heat, I think. This hot, close weather is putting everyone out of sorts. How lucky I am to be going to the seaside! I am very much looking forward to seeing you again.

Your loving sister, Jane.

To make the travelling easier for both ladies, it had been decided that Elizabeth would travel from Ramsgate to London with one of her aunt's servants. At the same time, Jane would travel from Longbourn to London with one of the Bennets' servants. Both young ladies would then spend the night at their aunt and uncle's house in London, to give them a break in their long journey. On the following day, Jane would travel on to Ramsgate with her aunt's servant, and Elizabeth would return to Longbourn with the Bennets' servant.

Thus, both ladies would be properly escorted and both servants would end up in their own establishments.

Elizabeth was looking forward to seeing Jane. It would be fun to spend the night with her in London. It would give them both a chance to catch up with all the latest news. Letters were agreeable, but not nearly as good as talking face to face. But even so, she was sorry to leave Ramsgate. She had spent a very pleasant two weeks there. She had enjoyed all the seaside activities, and she had particularly enjoyed her friendship with Georgiana.

The two of them were dissimilar personalities, but this had strengthened their friendship rather than hindered it. Elizabeth was far more confident and outspoken than Georgiana, but Georgiana was more demure than Elizabeth. Each had gained something from the other. Elizabeth had become more elegant and learnt more poise. Georgiana had become more confident and outgoing. She had also become less afraid of Mrs Younge and more ready to assert herself if she felt something was amiss.

Mr Wickham had continued to call on Georgiana, but if Elizabeth was present then he cut his visit short. He was always affable to Elizabeth, but there was something wary about him whenever she was near.

She was glad that Georgiana had written to her brother, informing him of Mr Wickham's presence in Ramsgate, because she felt that Mr

Darcy would know how to handle the situation and how to discourage Mr Wickham. She was only surprised that he had not done anything about it already. But she knew that gentlemen often had urgent business to attend to, and could not always use their time as they wished. However, there was nothing more she could do. The matter was now out of her hands.

Elizabeth folded Jane's letter and put it away. Then she donned her pelisse, gloves and bonnet, for she was engaged to take tea with Georgiana for one last time before she returned to London on the morrow. Taking her aunt's maid with her, she walked along the promenade, with the wind ruffling the hem of her muslin gown delightfully, and made the most of the view. The sea was looking particularly beautiful this morning, being as blue as the sky, with jaunty fishing boats dotting the waves. Seagulls soared high overhead, streaks of white against the blue, and filled the air with their cry.

She was soon at Georgiana's lodgings. But when she was admitted to the house, she heard raised voices coming from the drawing-room. The first voice was that of a man, but it was not a voice she recognised. It was not Mr Wickham's voice, it was another gentleman. The voice was refined and cultured. It had a deep resonance and was very attractive. But the words were far from being attractive.

' . . . I have been sadly deceived by you, Mrs

Younge. You have not only allowed Mr Wickham to call —'

'But, Sir, he claimed to be your friend, and Miss Darcy herself said she had grown up with him. I only —'

'Not only have you allowed Mr Wickham to call, you have also allowed Miss Darcy to befriend a most unsuitable young woman,' continued the gentleman. 'Upon enquiry, I found she was nothing but the daughter of one of the gentry – a most unsuitable friend for Miss Darcy of Pemberley.'

'But Fitzwilliam —' began Georgiana.

'You must allow me to decide who is and who isn't a suitable companion for you,' he said firmly. 'In fact, I think you have been in Ramsgate long enough, Georgiana. Oh, pray don't look so downcast, I do not wish to upset you, but it is time for you to come home. I will instruct your servants to pack your things and I will take you to London myself tomorrow morning. We must be ready to leave by ten o'clock.'

He turned and saw Elizabeth, who stood in the doorway.

'And you are Miss Bennet, I suppose,' he said, looking her up and down with a haughty air.

'I am,' she said, dropping him a curtsey before drawing herself up to her full height in order to meet his look.

He was, she noticed, extremely handsome. Dark hair framed a strong face with a determined jaw. His eyes were a velvety brown but they were, at the moment, filled with contempt. His clothes showed evidence of expensive tailoring, for they fit him like a second skin. His black coat moulded itself to his shoulders, his white shirt was ruffled at the front and at the wrist, and his cream breeches disappeared into highly polished boots.

'Miss Darcy will not be requiring your presence,' he said.

Georgiana gasped in dismay, but Elizabeth merely raised her eyebrows.

'I think that is for Miss Darcy to say,' she replied.

'I am her brother —'

'That fact had not escaped my notice,' said Elizabeth, interrupting him as he had interrupted everyone else.

'And you are a most unsuitable friend,' he finished scathingly.

'I am a gentleman's daughter,' returned Elizabeth with a lift of her chin. 'And as Miss Darcy is a gentleman's daughter, we are alike.'

'Nevertheless, Miss Darcy has no more need of your services. I will bid you good day.'

Elizabeth felt her anger growing at his terrible rudeness and by his description of her friendship as "services", as though she were a servant who could be dismissed. But seeing that the argument was distressing Georgiana, she disdained to bandy words with him. Instead, she dropped a haughty curtsey with her chin held high. Then she turned on her heel and swept out of the room.

'Well!' said her aunt's maid, as she followed Elizabeth out of the house. 'Of all the cheek.'

She had stood there with her mouth open in astonishment as Mr Darcy had delivered his autocratic speech.

'Mr Darcy needs a lesson in manners,' said Elizabeth angrily. 'Let us hope his sister can teach him some.'

'And you not even having a chance to say goodbye to Miss Darcy,' said her aunt's maid.

But, as to that, Elizabeth had her own ideas. She did not mean to leave Ramsgate without bidding her friend goodbye. Mr Darcy had told his sister to be ready to leave by ten o'clock the following morning and Elizabeth intended to call before then to bid Georgiana adieu. She would have time to do it before she herself was compelled to leave for London.

And she would suggest that she and Georgiana should write to each other, whatever Mr Darcy might say.

Mr George Wickham was in his lodgings, playing cards with a group of seedy men. They had all removed their coats and were playing in their shirt sleeves. A buxom wench was serving them drinks and every now and then one of the men would slap her on the behind and make some rude remark.

Wickham was just about to lay down his hand when there came a rapid knock at the door and, without further ado, Mrs Younge entered the room.

Wickham was at once alert.

'I have to speak to you urgently,' she said.

Wickham took her by the elbow and guided her into the next room.

'I thought I told you never to visit me here,' he said. 'What is it? Has Miss Bennet made difficulties?'

'You don't need to worry about her. He's sent her about her business,' said Mrs Younge.

'He?' asked Wickham.

'Yes, he. Mr Darcy.'

'Darcy!' Wickham was horrified.

'The very same. He's just arrived. He sent Miss Bennet packing and I thought he was going to send me packing, too, but he's told me I can stay 'til we get back to London. He's taking Georgiana back with him tomorrow.'

Wickham went white.

'This will ruin everything,' he said. 'I must have her fortune. My debts are numerous and ever mounting. If I can't pay them, I am in serious trouble.'

'Then you'd better come for her early, before her brother takes her away. It's your only chance.'

'But I haven't a carriage —'

'Then you'd better hire one. He's determined to leave at ten o'clock, and if you're not away by then it will be too late.'

'I don't know if she's ready,' said Wickham, pacing the room and running his hand through his hair. 'She likes me, I know, but whether she is ready to run off with me —' He pursed his lips, thinking. 'You said that Mr Darcy sent Miss Bennet away?'

'That's right. Said she wasn't good enough for Miss Darcy. Quite upset Miss Darcy, it did, to see her friend treated so badly.'

'It might just work in my favour,' said Mr Wickham. 'If Darcy is behaving like an arrogant monster – which, of course, he is – then Georgiana will be more likely to go against him. She has a tender heart and she is always full of sympathy for anyone who is being badly treated. If she thinks I am being badly treated, so much the better.'

'Yes, that is the way to play it,' said Mrs Younge, nodding.

'You must play upon her tender feelings tonight. Do not speak against Darcy – that will turn her against us. But tell her that her brother is old fashioned and that his pride will cause a great deal of unnecessary unhappiness. Tell her how upset I will be if I cannot see her again. Persuade her to come and meet me, to say goodbye. Tell her it would be rude for her to go without seeing me again, in fact, tell her it would be an insult.'

He stopped to think, his brow furrowed in concentration.

'We must meet somewhere away from the house, for by now I am sure Darcy will have given instructions that I am not to be admitted.'

'Yes, he has.'

'Very well. Tell her that I will be walking along the promenade in the morning. I will be waiting with a carriage, in some secluded street along the route, and if I cannot persuade her to come with me willingly, then I must bundle her into it and take her off to the border.'

'It's a desperate plot,' said Mrs Younge dubiously.

'I am a desperate man,' he said. 'I must have her fortune or I am ruined. Can I rely on you? You will be well rewarded.'

Mrs Younge nodded.

'Very well. Go now. Prey on her weaknesses. Remind her of her fondness for me. Fill her head with romantic nonsense. Do whatever you must in order to get her to agree to meet with me, and the rest you can leave to me.'

Chapter Three

Elizabeth had packed her bags in preparation for her journey to London. She ate a good breakfast with her aunt, uncle and cousins. Her uncle was looking much better than when they had arrived. He had grown in strength and had a much healthier colour. The sea air had agreed with him, and he had become more energetic in recent days. Elizabeth knew that Jane's company would improve his condition even more, for who could not feel better with Jane?

Her little cousins, too, were looking forward to Jane's stay. Jane was a great favourite with them. Elizabeth was loved because she would play with them in their livelier games, but Jane was loved for her calm patience and her ability to see the best in people – a particularly welcome characteristic when the children had been told off and needed someone to restore their belief in their own goodness.

'You have a pleasant day for the journey,' said Uncle Gardiner.

'Yes, it couldn't be better,' Elizabeth agreed.

It was fine, but not too hot, which was a relief. She was to travel on the stagecoach and so the cooler weather would make the journey much more agreeable.

After their final embraces, Elizabeth set out with her aunt's maid as a chaperone. But she did not make her way to the coaching inn straight away. Instead, she turned her steps towards Georgiana's Ramsgate house, because she was determined to take a proper farewell of her friend.

She walked along the sea front and then turned left, heading towards the large and imposing house. She had not gone far when she saw a carriage travelling down the road at great speed. If it had been travelling more slowly she would not have noticed it, but her curiosity was aroused and she turned her head to watch it pass by. As she did so, she saw Georgiana sitting inside, looking white and frightened. Next to her was Mr Wickham, and in the seat opposite them was Mrs Younge.

Elizabeth and her maid exchanged anxious glances. Something was clearly wrong.

Elizabeth was closer now to Miss Darcy's house than her aunt's house, and so she decided to seek help at the nearer establishment. She hurried on, and when the footman opened the door, she said, 'I must speak to Mr Darcy at once. Is he within?'

The footman said, 'I'm sorry, miss, but I have orders not to admit you.'

'This is an urgent matter and I must insist,' said Elizabeth, stepping past him into the hall.

She looked up and saw that Mr Darcy was descending the stairs. His face became extremely arrogant when he saw her and he said, 'Miss

Bennet. I thought I made it clear —'

'I must speak to you on a matter of urgency,' said Elizabeth. 'It concerns Miss Darcy.'

She relied on him not wishing to make a scene in front of the servants. He looked displeased, but as he could not fail to notice the curious face of the footman, he said curtly, 'You had better come in.'

The footman opened the door to the drawing-room.

Elizabeth went in and Mr Darcy followed her.

He looked surprised to see that the room was empty and Elizabeth realised he had been expecting to see his sister there. But he quickly turned his attention to the matter in hand.

'Now, Miss Bennet,' he said, closing the door behind her and her maid. 'You have come, I suppose, to say that you are a suitable friend for Miss Darcy.'

'Insufferable man!' she said. 'I have come for nothing of the sort. I have just seen Miss Darcy in a carriage with Mr Wickham, heading out of town. Mrs Younge was with her but Miss Darcy looked frightened. I fear that Mr Wickham and Mrs Younge are in league and have abducted her.'

'What fairy tale is this?' he demanded.

But nevertheless, Elizabeth saw a hint of uncertainty in his eye and he glanced around the room again.

'It is not fairy tale. I beg you, there is not a moment to lose. I have suspected a connection between Mr Wickham and Mrs Younge for some time. Oh, make haste! Order your carriage! You can catch them yet!'

'The carriage has already been ordered for my journey to London,' he said. 'It will be at the door momentarily. If what you say is true . . . '

He looked at her maid, as if to ask for confirmation of Elizabeth's story, and the maid nodded.

'Tell me, which way were they headed?' asked Mr Darcy.

He was suddenly full of energy and Elizabeth felt a flood of relief as she knew he believed her.

'North, along the London road,' she said.

'Then he has designs on her fortune and they are headed to Scotland, to marry over the anvil at Gretna Green.' His brow furrowed in thought. 'You had better come with me,' he said decisively to Elizabeth. 'You seem to know a great deal, and I must know everything if I am to save Georgiana. If there has been some collusion between Mr Wickham and Mrs Younge as you say, then they might stop overnight and I need to know everything in case it helps me to discover where they will stop.'

'I cannot come with you!' said Elizabeth, horrified he should even suggest such a thing.

'On the contrary, you can and you must. You

were planning to travel to London today anyway, my sister said so.'

'Yes, I was, but —'

'Then you will travel there with me in my carriage, and along the way you will tell me everything I need to know.'

'It is most improper!' exclaimed Elizabeth.

'It is nothing of the kind. You have your maid with you to ensure your respectability, and as you are a friend of my sister, no one will think it odd that I should offer to take you to London when I am returning to London myself.'

'You were not so keen to claim me as a friend of your sister yesterday,' she remarked scathingly.

'That was different.'

'Because you did not need me then. Tell me, Mr Darcy, do you always use people in this shameful manner?'

'I do not have time to bandy words with you. Will you come with me or won't you?' he demanded.

She was tempted to give him a sharp set-down but she was concerned about Georgiana and she was willing to do anything she could to help her friend.

'Yes,' she said. 'I will.'

The footman entered the room.

'The carriage is ready, sir. You asked to be informed when it was at the door.'

'Good. Tell my valet he must follow me with

my valise on the stagecoach. I am in a hurry.' He turned to Elizabeth. 'Miss Bennet?'

He gave her his arm.

After a moment of surprise at this courtesy, she took it.

Her eyes widened as the contact produced a strange reaction in her. Heat radiated out from her hand where it rested on his arm.

She looked at him in surprise, but immediately looked away as she did not want him to know he had any effect on her. He was the proudest, most disagreeable man she had ever met, and the sooner his sister was found, the more pleased she would be, not just for Georgiana's sake, but because then she would be rid of Mr Darcy.

He escorted her out of the house, down the steps and into the carriage, with her aunt's maid following behind. He instructed the coachman to take the London road. The coachman's eyebrows lifted and it was evident he thought they would be waiting for Miss Darcy. But he said nothing and Elizabeth realised he knew better than to question Mr Darcy about a change of plan. The footman, too, said nothing, merely closed the door of the carriage behind them and returned to the house.

'Now,' said Mr Darcy, as he settled himself back against the squabs. 'You had better tell me everything. Hold nothing back. If you have been involved in this in any way, I will find out, so you had better tell me at once.'

'*Involved in it?*' demanded Elizabeth angrily. 'What do you take me for?'

'I take you for a young woman who has scraped an acquaintance with an heiress at a seaside resort,' he remarked.

'You are the most insufferable man I have ever met,' she said. 'Are you always so arrogant?'

'Arrogant?' he asked in surprise.

'Yes. Arrogant, high handed, contemptuous and supercilious,' she said with a spark in her eyes. 'You declared me to be an unsuitable friend for your sister when you knew nothing about me, and now you have the effrontery to imply that I might have had something to do with your sister's difficulties, when the fault lies squarely at your door.'

'Miss Bennet, you go too far,' he said, with an angry set of his mouth.

'I do not go far enough. You sent your sister down to Ramsgate with only a companion and a few servants to protect her and keep her company, and then you wonder why she was vulnerable to the charms of a man like George Wickham!'

'Charms?' he said in disgust.

'Yes, charms!' she declared. 'Georgiana —'

'Miss Darcy to you!' he said.

'Georgiana,' she said firmly, 'is at an impressionable age. If a good looking man, with a good address, takes an interest in her and pays her compliments then of course she is going to regard him favourably, especially if he is an old family friend.'

'He is nothing of the kind!'

'As I have come to realise,' said Elizabeth. She had suspected as much and Mr Darcy's behaviour showed her that she had been right. 'But if he is not an old family friend then why did Georgiana think he was? She must have had some reason for it.'

'He was once admitted to our family circle,' Mr Darcy conceded. 'He was the son of my father's steward and we grew up together. But he turned out wild and it is now some time since I have thought of him as a friend. He refused to apply himself to any profession and I washed my hands of him. Georgiana was well aware of it. Mr Wickham and I have not been friends for years.'

'But it was not hard for him to persuade her otherwise,' said Elizabeth. 'What more natural than that a loving young lady, such as your sister is, should hope for a reconciliation and see it as inevitable when it happened? I doubt if Georgiana has ever held a grudge in her life.'

'No. In that we are different, for my good opinion, once lost, is lost forever,' he said, almost to himself.

'That is very harsh,' said Elizabeth in surprise.

He turned deep-set eyes on her and she saw that once again they were filled with a haughty disdain. They said, more clearly than words, *Who are you to judge me? Me, Fitzwilliam Darcy?*

But Elizabeth was not quelled. She had a strong spirit, and it rose to every challenge.

'A world without forgiveness would be a very hard place to live in. If every wrong is to be held against us forever, then what hope is there for any of us? We are none of us without fault.'

Mr Darcy did not reply, he merely looked at her with arrogant eyes.

'But perhaps you are without fault,' she said challengingly.

She wanted to pierce his arrogant armour and humble his pride. She had never met anyone like him before. He was so certain of everything, and she was sure he had never doubted himself or his opinions in his life.

And why should he? Brought up as a rich and powerful man, surrounded by lackeys who agreed with him all the time, and with only a younger sister who was in awe of him, there was no one to keep his pride in check.

In her own household, such pomposity would not have survived for five minutes. It would have been pricked before it had time to take root. But Mr Darcy, with no parents, and with a sister who was so much younger than him . . . Mr Darcy had no one to puncture his conceit.

'We are none of us without fault,' he said at last.

But he said it in such a way that it was clear he thought he did not have any faults, whatever he might say.

'Then you, also, must have faults. Do you hope to correct them, and to be forgiven for them? Or do you perhaps think they are so insignificant that you do not need to correct them? Or perhaps you have such a low opinion of everyone else that you do not care if they are forgiven or not. Perhaps your own good opinion is sufficient for you.'

'You seem to have a very decided view of me on such a short acquaintance,' he remarked in some agitation.

She was glad to have pierced his armour, even in a small way.

'Sometimes, a short acquaintance is enough.' Her thoughts went to her first sight of Mr Wickham, bowing over Georgiana's hand. 'I knew that Mr Wickham was not to be trusted the moment I set eyes on him. There was something abut his manner which was overly familiar, and when Miss Darcy tried to introduce him to me, he interrupted her and took the introduction into his own hands.'

'So that he could give a good account of himself, no doubt.'

Elizabeth nodded.

'He introduced himself as a friend of the

family,' she said.

'Whereas he is nothing of the kind. I thought only of Georgiana's health and happiness when I sent her to Ramsgate. I did not know Wickham would follow her here!'

'No, and you would never have known, if I had not advised your sister to tell you about it in her next letter.'

'*You* advised her to tell me?' he asked in surprise.

'Yes. I had no right to tell her what to do, and so I could not tell her to forbid him the house, but I was suspicious of his attentions and I was sure you would like to know that he was here. So I suggested she mention his presence in her next letter. I felt sure you would know what to do about it.'

'And so I did,' he said. 'I made arrangements to visit her as soon as her letter arrived. Unfortunately the letter was delayed, or else I would have been here sooner. But I did not know that I had you to thank for the information.'

'That is hardly surprising, since you did not give me a chance to speak. You bustled me out of the house yesterday as if I were a beggar. Worse, for even a beggar at my house would be treated with some civility.'

He scowled, but by the way he shifted uncomfortably in his seat, she could tell her remark had hit home.

With his next breath he tried to justify his conduct.

'My sister has been the object of unscrupulous people in the past, who have scraped an acquaintance with her in order to ingratiate themselves with my family,' he said. 'It has been my duty to protect her from such impertinences.'

'And so, because there are some unscrupulous people in the world, everyone who speaks to your sister must be suspect?' demanded Elizabeth.

By now he had recovered his aplomb. He turned superior eyes on her and said, 'Yes, they must. I would rather offend a stranger than expose my sister to the false friendships of those who seek to use her for their own purposes.'

'Then, if you are going to be so severe, it would be as well to be certain of your facts before subjecting innocent people to your disapproval,' she said, her eyes flashing.

'And in the meantime?' he demanded. 'Is my sister to suffer the pangs of betrayal when she discovers that her new friends are nothing of the sort, but are merely people who are using her for their own ends? It is better for me to be suspicious to begin with, and save her that pain. There is time enough for friendships to develop when I have vetted her new acquaintance.'

'Then I hope you will find some people you think suitable quickly,' Elizabeth flashed back.

'Your sister is lonely. She is pining for female companionship of her own age. It is not enough to give her a large house and beautiful clothes and an array of servants. She must have friends or she will be poor indeed.'

Mr Darcy's pride had been growing throughout this speech.

'It is not your place to lecture me on the way I look after my sister,' he exploded, his dark eyes flashing with outrage.

'Well, someone must do it, and if you are as high-handed with everyone else as you are with me, I dare say they are too cowed to tell you anything you do not wish to hear,' remarked Elizabeth, refusing to be cowed. 'And few people, I dare say, would be brave enough to tell you the same thing twice. But it is your sister who is suffering. She needs young ladies with whom she can discuss fashions and bonnets and music and romance.'

'She is far too young to be thinking about romance,' said Mr Darcy curtly.

'Apparently not, since Mr Wickham was able to win her affection so easily,' returned Elizabeth pointedly.

He had no answer for that and so he fell into a brooding silence. His fine cheekbones were etched and his jaw was set as he looked out of the window, his dark eyes full of turmoil. His shoulders were held straight, but she could tell it was an effort for him not to slump in his distress.

He set one booted foot on the raised edge of the door and he rested his elbow on his knee. The black of his tailcoat showed up in stark contrast to the white of his breeches, and he drummed his fingers against the window in frustration.

Elizabeth despised Mr Darcy for his rudeness, but she could not help pitying his distress. He was a good brother even if he was misguided, because it was clear he loved Georgiana very much.

At last the coach turned off the road and clattered into the yard of a coaching inn.

'Wait here,' he said to Elizabeth as it drew to a halt.

Without giving her a chance to reply, he jumped out of the carriage and went to consult the ostlers about any other carriages which had just passed through.

He rejoined Elizabeth a few minutes later.

'They have been here,' he said. 'They changed horses and sped off again, but we have been making good time and we are now not more than five or ten minutes behind them. We will soon catch them.'

The coach set off again at a riotous pace. Since the horses were still fresh, and since Mr Darcy intended to overtake his sister in a few miles, he had not taken the time to have his own horses changed.

He said no more to Elizabeth. Instead, he resumed his former brooding attitude.

Elizabeth turned to look out of the window in an effort to catch sight of Wickham's carriage. But Mr Darcy was reflected in the carriage window, and she found herself tracing his face with her eyes in an effort to work him out.

His character was a complex one. Even on such a short acquaintance, she had seen many contradictions in it. He was a proud and arrogant man, and yet his affection for his sister was real and sincere. Moreover, it revealed a softer side of his character. She wondered what that softer side would be like and regretted that she would not have a chance to find out, for he would never show it to Miss Elizabeth Bennet. Who was Miss Elizabeth Bennet, after all? In the opinion of Mr Darcy she was no one at all. And so she would never see anything of him except his proud and haughty exterior.

The coach turned a bend and there, ahead of her, she saw a carriage she recognised.

'It is them!' she exclaimed.

Mr Darcy told the coachman to push the horses harder, and soon the coach drew level with Mr Wickham's carriage.

The coachman, an expert driver, pressed Mr Wickham's carriage hard and forced it off the road.

Mr Wickham's coachman cursed but no one paid him any attention.

Mr Darcy leapt out of the coach, closely followed by Elizabeth, and flung open the door of Mr Wickham's carriage.

Elizabeth's heart went out to Georgiana. From the state of her dress it was obvious what had happened. Mr Wickham had attempted to ruin Georgiana so that Mr Darcy would agree to a marriage after all.

Luckily, Elizabeth and Mr Darcy had caught Mr Wickham in time, and although Georgiana was upset, no damage had been done.

As Mr Darcy caught Mr Wickham by the lapels and dragged him out of the coach, where he felled him with one well-placed punch, Georgiana collapsed into Elizabeth's arms.

'Hush,' said Elizabeth. 'You are safe now. There is no harm done.'

There was a hint of a question in her voice, and Georgiana shook her head. 'He kissed me, but he had time for no more. Oh! To think how I once dreamed of his kisses! But he was not the man who courted me. That man was polite and charming and full of deference. The man who abducted me was another man entirely, a desperate villain who would stop at nothing to gain his own ends. How can one man have two such different faces?'

'You are very young,' said Elizabeth soothingly. 'You will soon learn to tell the difference between a good man and a bad one, and your brother will be more careful of your companions in future, for it is clear Mrs Younge must have been involved.'

'Yes,' said Georgiana, as her sobs subsided. 'She knew Mr Wickham and they arranged it together.'

Elizabeth put her arm around Georgiana and led her towards the coach.

As she did so, she heard Mr Wickham say, 'If you mention this to anyone, Darcy, I will say that Georgiana came willingly and I will ruin her reputation.'

Elizabeth saw that Mr Darcy was controlling himself with great difficulty, but his pride had got the better of his anger and he did not knock Mr Wickham down again.

'If you ever say one word against Georgiana, I will destroy you,' said Mr Darcy, his face white with anger. 'I will make sure that nowhere in England will hold you.' He turned to Mrs Younge. 'And as for you, Ma'am, you will never again work for a decent family. You have betrayed your trust and you are lucky I don't take you before the magistrate. But I will make sure you never again have a young lady in your charge. Now be gone, the pair of you, before I change my mind about letting you go.'

Mr Wickham and Mrs Younge picked themselves up and climbed hurriedly back into their carriage.

Mr Darcy approached and Georgiana shrank from him, too ashamed to go to him. But Mr Darcy held out his hands to her and then she flew to him like a bird, burying her face in his coat. His strong arms closed around her and she sobbed on his chest.

'So there is some forgiveness in you, after all,' said Elizabeth softly.

But Mr Darcy turned a hard gaze on Elizabeth and said, 'Georgiana was not at fault. There is nothing to forgive. It is Mr Wickham and Mrs Younge who were at fault, and I will never forgive them.'

He led Georgiana back to the coach, comforting her all the while.

Elizabeth followed them, with her aunt's maid bringing up the rear.

Mr Darcy gave Elizabeth an uncomprehending look when she climbed into the coach and she realised with a shock that, now he had no further use for her, he did not expect her to go any further with him.

Her spirit rose at once.

'Perhaps you would prefer I walk to London?' she asked defiantly, smarting from his look.

A frown crossed his face. He hesitated for a brief moment and then said grudgingly, 'No, that will not be necessary.'

'That is very good of you,' she said, with a haughty gaze of her own. 'How kind of you not to expect me to walk for fifty miles or more. Now, if you would be good enough to take me to Gracechurch Street, I would be much obliged,' she said.

Mr Darcy's look of disgust conveyed his views on Gracechurch Street. It was a respectable address, but it was not in a fashionable part of town, and it was inhabited by men of business and not by men of any great social standing. Nevertheless, Mr Darcy gave his coachman instructions to take them there, and they were soon on their way again.

The rest of the journey was completed in silence.

Georgiana, exhausted from her ordeal, sank against her brother's chest.

Mr Darcy, his face stony, appeared to be thinking about what he would like to do to Mr Wickham if he were not too much of a gentleman to do it.

Elizabeth's maid did not like to speak.

And Elizabeth's mind was too full of everything that had happened to allow her to say anything.

When at last the coach turned into Gracechurch Street, Elizabeth took a subdued leave of the Darcys. Georgiana turned her head and attempted a smile, but she was clearly still shocked and not capable of anything more.

Mr Darcy did not even climb out of the coach in order to hand Elizabeth down. He merely made her a slight bow as she bid him farewell.

Never had she been made to feel more insignificant.

As she heard the coach pulling away she

thought that, if not for the friendship she bore Georgiana, she would have been very happy never to hear the name of Darcy again.

She crossed the pavement to the steps leading up to her aunt's front door. As she did so, she happened to look up and saw Jane's face at the window above.

She gave a huge sigh of relief. It was a most welcome sight! She felt lighter of heart just seeing her sister, and the world seemed a friendly place again. A smile crossed her tired and careworn face.

'Oh, Jane, I am so glad you are here before me,' she said, as she went into the house and removed her bonnet in the hall.

She embraced her sister, holding her tightly for longer than usual.

Jane pulled back, still holding Lizzy's hands, and looked at her in surprise.

'Why, Lizzy, whatever has happened? I saw you arriving in a private coach, instead of walking from the coaching inn as I had expected. Who did it belong to?'

'Oh, Jane,' said Elizabeth, as the two ladies went into the drawing-room. 'What a lot I have to tell you!'

Chapter Four

'I cannot believe it,' said Jane.

She and Elizabeth were sitting in the drawing-room. Elizabeth had had time to recover from her strange day. She had removed her outdoor clothes and she had had a pot of tea, together with a light supper prepared by her aunt's servant. She had very much needed the refreshment. The journey had been long, some eighty miles or thereabouts. It had taken most of the day, even in Mr Darcy's superior carriage with the horses being frequently changed. They had eaten a hurried luncheon at one of the coaching inns but that had been Elizabeth's only chance for food.

'It is true, nonetheless,' said Elizabeth.

'That a gentleman should be so lost to all decency that he would abduct a gently born young lady, and, from what you say, a delightful one,' said Jane, horrified.

'Mr Wickham is no gentleman,' said Elizabeth with a shake of her head. 'He has all the appearance of one, but he has the manners of a scoundrel.'

'Thank goodness you saw the carriage and were able to alert Mr Darcy,' said Jane.

'Yes – for all the thanks I had,' said Elizabeth.

'It was very wrong of him to treat you so badly, although he thought he was doing the best for his sister.'

'Dear Jane!' said Elizabeth with a smile. 'Always seeing the best in people! Mr Darcy knew very well he was being rude and disagreeable – or, if he didn't, he should have done! He is not deficient in intellect and he must have had a good education. There is no excuse for him.'

'Never mind,' said Jane with a sympathetic smile. 'You will not have to see him again.'

'No, for which I am truly grateful. And yet I am concerned about Georgiana. She was very upset and said scarcely a word. She has no friends of her own age and I am worried about her. Do you think I should call?'

Jane hesitated.

'Yes, I know,' said Elizabeth, reading Jane's mind. 'Were Miss Darcy not so high, I would call as a matter of course. But if I arrive at the Darcys' London house uninvited, I fear I will not be admitted.'

'You could write to her,' said Jane. 'I think you said Miss Darcy gave you the name of her London home?'

Elizabeth brightened.

'Yes, she did. That is a very good notion, I will write at once,' she said. 'It will set my mind at rest to know she has recovered from her ordeal.'

She went over to the writing desk and pulled forward a sheet of paper and a quill. She dipped the quill in the ink and began to write, expressing her concern. Then she gave it to the servant to deliver.

'And now, tell me all the news from home,' she said.

After giving Elizabeth news of all the family, Jane said, 'Netherfield Park is to be let.'

Elizabeth's interest was caught. The owner had recently died and his heirs had decided to rent it out, for they already had their own estate and did not need another one to live in.

'Has there been any interest in it?' asked Elizabeth.

'Yes, several people have been to view it, although, so far, no one has taken it. But it is only a matter of time. Mama is very excited about it. She hopes it will be taken by a large family with plenty of sons. In fact, she talks of little else.'

'Poor Papa!' said Elizabeth with a laugh.

'Yes,' said Jane. 'He is already tired of the subject, but I fear that nothing will stop Mama. He will be very pleased to have you home again.'

'And I will be very pleased to be there. Despite its trials, it is still home, and after my eventful summer, I will be glad to return to more familiar irritations. If only I can hear from Miss Darcy before I go back to Longbourn, I will be able leave the Darcys and their problems behind.'

Mr Darcy stood by the fireplace of Georgiana's London establishment, drumming his fingers on the mantelpiece. He had given her into the care of her London maid, explaining her distraught state by saying there had been a carriage accident, and advising that she be put to bed.

He had sent a note to his cousin, Colonel Fitzwilliam, immediately on returning to London, asking him to call. Colonel Fitzwilliam was Georgiana's joint guardian, with Mr Darcy, and Mr Darcy wanted to tell him of the situation.

Colonel Fitzwilliam soon arrived and the two men discussed what they should do.

Colonel Fitzwilliam was all for horsewhipping Mr Wickham, but gradually he became calmer and the two gentlemen agreed that any dramatic action would draw attention to the incident. And that was something they wanted to avoid.

'I blame myself,' said Mr Darcy. 'I should not have sent her to Ramsgate alone.'

'Hardly alone,' protested Colonel Fitzwilliam. 'She had a companion and a complement of servants. You were not to blame.'

'No?' said Mr Darcy.

Miss Elizabeth Bennet's words returned to him and cut him on the raw.

'Regardless, it is done now and there is no undoing it,' said Colonel Fitzwilliam. 'Let us be thankful that nothing worse happened, and that

Georgiana will soon recover.'

'Yes, let us hope so. I mean to take her to Pemberley with me as soon as possible.'

'A good idea,' said Colonel Fitzwilliam. 'Get her out in the fresh air, riding and walking. It will banish her troubles more quickly than staying indoors. And invite some agreeable company. She has had a shock and you do not want her to become afraid of men. Charles Bingley is a good sort of man, why not invite him to Pemberley? His gentle manners will soon restore her faith in life.'

'I have been thinking much the same thing myself,' said Mr Darcy. 'And I will invite his sisters, too. Georgiana needs some female company.'

It had not occurred to him before. He had seen Georgiana as a child still, who would be content with her needlework and her music, but Miss Elizabeth Bennet was right. Georgiana was growing up and she was thinking, naturally, of clothes and romance, as well as her accomplishments. She was too young yet to be out in society, but this did not mean that she had to be treated as a child in all things. Some concessions must be made to the fact that she was a young lady and no longer a little girl.

Colonel Fitzwilliam took his leave, and Mr Darcy attended to some small matters of business which had arisen while he had been away.

The mail was laid on a silver salver, as usual, and once he had attended to his other business he picked up the first letter. It had been delivered by hand. It was addressed to his sister and, as he did not recognise the writing, he opened it, for he was determined to protect her from any possible distress.

He glanced down the page to the signature and saw it was from Miss Elizabeth Bennet.

He squirmed inwardly. He was not comfortable thinking about that young woman. He was aware that he owed her a great deal, for without Miss Elizabeth's timely warning, Georgiana might have eloped with George Wickham. And if not for Miss Elizabeth seeing Wickham's carriage, Georgiana would have been successfully abducted by him. If that had happened, there would have been endless complications, as well as all the distress and degradation it would have occasioned for Georgiana.

But although he owed Miss Elizabeth a great deal, he knew her to be far beneath him – and far beneath his sister – and he did not want to encourage her.

His sense of justice here warred with his sense of pride. On the one hand, he should thank her and invite her to tea with Georgiana. On the other hand, he felt that the sooner the disastrous Ramsgate chapter of his sister's life was closed, the better.

And then there were his own feelings, barely acknowledged, to consider. He had been affronted when Miss Elizabeth had argued with him, but he had also been attracted. No one else had the courage to speak to him in the way she had spoken to him and it had been strangely appealing. She had made him view her as a strong-minded person, instead of a humble worshipper at his feet. She was intelligent and had a great deal of insight into his sister. Insight he lacked. Because, although he loved his sister, he was a man, and he could not understand the finer points of the female psyche. But now, thanks to Miss Elizabeth, he realised there were things that Georgiana needed, and he meant to give them to her in the form of more female friends. He also meant to treat her like a young lady instead of a little girl as he had a greater appreciation of the fact that she was growing up.

For all this, he had to thank Miss Elizabeth.

But he was resentful rather than grateful.

He hated to acknowledge the fact to himself, but it was so. He would rather view her as a person of no consequence but she had forced him to see her differently, and Mr Darcy was not used to being forced into things.

Nor did he like the experience.

He remembered the way her eyes had sparked and her cheeks had flushed with the force of her arguments, and the way it had made his body react. The way, too, it had made his mind and spirit react. She had a way of challenging him which was not pleasant, but was not altogether unpleasant either, and even in a very short space of time she had made an impact on him.

He did not wish her to make any further impact on him, because he already found it difficult to forget her and, in particular, to forget the expression in her eyes. They were beautifully shaped and very fine. If he saw her again, he believed he might be in danger of treating her with more attention than she deserved. He really ought to forget her.

But this left him in an awkward position. Should he give Georgiana leave to invite Miss Elizabeth to tea or not?

To his surprise, he felt a stab of pleasure at the thought of Miss Elizabeth sitting in his home, and he felt a longing to see her face again. But against that was set a desire to end the Ramsgate incident, both for himself and for his sister.

In the end, the latter desire won.

He went over to his writing desk and penned a brief letter to Miss Elizabeth Bennet, thanking her for her concern and telling her that Georgiana was now safely in the bosom of her own family and recovering from the disagreeable incident.

The letter made it clear that Miss Elizabeth Bennet should not write to Miss Darcy again.

He signed it with a flourish, then folded the

paper and sealed it.

He rang the bell, knowing that the footman who answered it would be discreet. This footman had been sent on delicate errands before and would not think it odd that he was being sent to Gracechurch Street. Or, at least, if he thought it odd, he would not comment on it. Neither would he gossip about it, for he was loyal to the Darcy family.

Mr Darcy handed him the letter. The footman took it, bowed and withdrew.

Then Mr Darcy set about banishing Miss Elizabeth Bennet from his mind.

Elizabeth and Jane spent a friendly evening together. Jane wanted to know all about Ramsgate, for Elizabeth had not yet told her about the town and the seaside as she had been too busy telling her about the Darcys. But now that Elizabeth had confided in Jane about the remarkable incidents, she was able to tell Jane all about the more normal side of her stay. She told Jane where the best haberdasher's was, so that Jane could buy pins and ribbons and any other little things she might need during her stay. She told her where the best dress shops were, so that Jane could enjoy looking at the expensive creations in the window, though such gowns were beyond their means. She told her which milliners stocked the best bonnets, for she knew that Jane needed a new one. And when she had finished telling Jane about the shops, she told her about the beach, how it ran for miles with a flat promenade to walk on and a sparkling blue sea. She talked of paddling and sea bathing – for there were bathing machines on the beach, and Elizabeth had several times ventured into the water. And then she spoke of her aunt and uncle, their kindness and her uncle's improving health. She told Jane about the children, and how much they were enjoying their holiday, with its paddling and kite flying and sea bathing and trips to local beauty spots for picnics. So that by the time she had finished, Jane was well prepared for her holiday and looking forward to it.

Elizabeth had just convinced herself she had forgotten all about the Darcys when she saw a footman walking proudly along the street outside. She stopped talking in mid-sentence.

'What is it?' asked Jane.

'That is one of Mr Darcy's footmen,' said Elizabeth.

'See, Lizzy, Mr Darcy is not as bad as you think him,' said Jane in her friendly and forgiving manner. 'He is no doubt going to invite you to tea.'

'Perhaps,' said Elizabeth dubiously.

There came a knock at the door and their aunt's servant answered it. A minute or two later, they saw the footman leaving.

'He has not waited for a reply,' said

Elizabeth. 'That does not bode well.'

The servant brought the letter in and handed it to Elizabeth with a curtsey.

'Thank you, that will be all,' said Elizabeth.

She did not want the servant to guess that anything unusual had happened.

When the servant had left the room, Elizabeth examined the letter. It was written in a clear, bold masculine hand.

Elizabeth read the contents with ever-growing impatience.

'Impossible man!' she said.

'What does it say?' asked Jane.

'See for yourself,' she said, handing the letter to Jane.

'Oh, dear,' said Jane, when she had finished the letter.

Even her gentle nature could not find anything good to say about it.

'It is my dismissal,' said Elizabeth. 'He could not have been more rude or condescending if I had been an unsatisfactory servant who was being sent on her way.'

'Oh, Lizzy,' said Jane sympathetically. 'It was a very bad letter, I agree.'

Elizabeth's face softened and she stretched out her hand to her sister, who took it with a friendly squeeze.

'If even you cannot think of anything good to say about the letter, then it must be very rude indeed!' she said. 'Well, what do I care? The

Darcys are nothing to me. I liked Georgiana very much and I am sorry for her, but I can do nothing about it. And so let us forget them. I have done with the Darcys. I am fortunate to be with my own family, and I take comfort from the fact that I will never have to see Mr Darcy again.'

Chapter Five

August passed and September arrived. Mr Darcy spent the time at Pemberley with his sister. He watched over her carefully and anything he could do for her pleasure, he did. He engaged a new companion for her, a motherly woman by the name of Mrs Annesley. He invited his aunt, Lady Catherine de Bourgh, and her daughter, Miss Anne de Bourgh, in the hope their company would help to lift Georgiana's spirits. And he invited Mr Bingley, together with Mr Bingley's two sisters. But although Georgiana played duets with Miss Bingley, and sang with Mrs Hurst, and took turns around the park in a pretty little phaeton with Miss Anne de Bourgh, she remained downcast. So much so, that Mr Darcy became concerned. He consulted the family physician (although he did not reveal the cause of Georgiana's low spirits) and the physician advised a change of scene.

'Perhaps some sea air,' that worthy man said.

Mr Darcy shuddered, knowing that the seaside was the last place Georgiana needed to be. But a change of scene seemed a good idea. Mr Bingley was thinking of renting a country estate, and Mr Darcy thought that, once Mr Bingley's estate was rented, he would take Georgiana with him on a visit.

It took Mr Bingley some time to find an estate he liked, but at last he settled on a place in Hertfordshire. He was delighted when Mr Darcy accepted his invitation to stay, and he readily extended the invitation to include Georgiana.

Elizabeth had settled into life at Longbourn once more. Her mother was insufferable for the first few weeks after she returned from Ramsgate, bemoaning the fact that neither she nor Jane had returned home with a husband-to-be. But Elizabeth was used to her mother's complaints and she bore it well. Her life resumed its familiar course, with visits to her Aunt Philips and walks into Meryton. But one morning, everything changed when Mrs Bennet came into the drawing-room with a faced wreathed in smiles.

'Netherfield Park is let!' said Mrs Bennet. 'Mrs Long has just been here and told me all about it. Even better, it has been taken by a man of large fortune from the north of England. A Mr Bingley. And what do you think? He is single!'

Mr Bennet displayed very little interest at the news, but Lydia was suitably impressed.

'He might marry me!' she said.

'I am sure he might, since your sisters are in no hurry to find a husband. You, Lydia, I am persuaded, are far more sensible, and will not waste your chances.'

'What fun it would be, to be married before either of you!' said Lydia to Elizabeth and Jane.

'He might marry me,' said Kitty.

'In point of fact, he is unlikely to marry anyone from the neighbourhood,' said Mary in a moralising tone. 'He will likely choose a young woman from the north of England, and he will no doubt require her to have a handsome dowry. No one in Meryton will suit him.'

Mrs Bennet ignored Mary, as always.

'Jane, Lizzy, come with me,' she said. 'We must look over your wardrobes. If I can but see one of my daughters happily settled at Netherfield, and all the others equally well married, I shall have nothing to wish for.'

Elizabeth and Jane exchanged long-suffering glances, but nevertheless they followed their mother from the room. They knew there was no way to stop her from matchmaking, and so they resigned themselves to her fussing over them, and they bore it with a good grace.

'Well, Darcy, have I not found a fine place?' asked Mr Bingley, as he looked round the drawing-room at Netherfield Park with satisfaction. It was a handsome room, with tall windows letting in the early autumn sunlight. There were three sofas arranged around the fireplace and there were padded window seats covered in gold damask. There were side tables and several upright chairs made out of mahogany. The walls were painted a pale cream with white mouldings, giving the whole room an elegant feel.

'You have done very well,' Mr Darcy agreed.

He had travelled from Pemberley the day before, bringing Georgiana with him. So far, she had not seemed to benefit from the change, but it was early days and Mr Darcy still hoped the visit would do her some good.

'It is not as fine as Pemberley, of course,' said Caroline Bingley, Charles's sister.

She was a tall, elegant woman, dressed in a wine-coloured silk gown. Her hair was arranged in an elaborate style, and she wore rubies at her throat.

'But then, where is?' asked Louisa Hurst, Charles's other, married sister.

She, too, was a very elegant woman, though not so tall as her sister. Her clothes, too, were very fine and her gown was made of green silk.

'It is very pleasant, even so, is it not, Georgiana?' asked Mr Darcy, drawing his sister into the conversation.

'Yes,' she said.

'And my neighbours are most agreeable,' said Mr Bingley. 'They called on me at the earliest opportunity. There was a Sir William Lucas —'

'Who tried to impress us with his talk of St James's Palace,' said Caroline, laughing in a sneering way.

'And Mr Bennet —'

'A typical country gentleman, with no

fashion or refinement,' said Caroline.

But Mr Darcy was not listening to Caroline. He had been struck by the name of Bennet and he looked at his sister. She, too, had been struck by it, and for the first time since leaving Ramsgate she seemed alert. She looked towards Mr Bingley with real interest and Mr Darcy's heart swelled to see it. His sister had been so quiet and withdrawn in recent weeks that he had been concerned for her wellbeing, and he had begun to wonder if she would ever get over her ordeal.

'And a great many other people besides,' said Mr Bingley.

'When are we to meet them?' asked Mr Darcy.

'At the Meryton assembly,' said Mr Bingley. 'If you remember, I mentioned it to you. It is to be held tomorrow night.'

'Do not feel obliged to attend,' said Caroline Bingley. 'I cannot think a country assembly will afford you any great pleasure, Mr Darcy.'

'On the contrary. I am looking forward to it,' said Mr Darcy, surprising everyone in the room.

'Good, that is settled then. We will go as a party,' said Mr Bingley.

Alone in his room later that night, Mr Darcy had a chance to think over the present situation and he found that his feelings were mixed. He had not forgotten Miss Elizabeth Bennet, despite his best efforts, and although his memories were not all pleasant, they had nevertheless made a lasting impression.

She had made a lasting impression on his sister, too, if Georgiana's reaction to the name Bennet was anything to go by.

Of course, it might not be the same family. But there was a chance that it was, and that Mr Bingley had moved into Miss Elizabeth Bennet's neighbourhood.

Mr Darcy was not sure how he felt about it. He did not like Miss Elizabeth Bennet. No, most assuredly he did not. She had not treated him with the deference that was due to Mr Darcy of Pemberley. He felt himself bristle as he thought about it. His pride was aroused, even just by thinking of her, and it had been ten times worse when he had been in her company. She had spoken to him as she might speak to a butcher or baker or candlestick maker. And yet there had been something about her that compelled his respect, and despite his best efforts to forget her, he had not been able to do so. He still thought about her at the most surprising moments. He would be talking about something quite different, and a little thing that someone said or did would remind him of her. Or he would be walking in the park at Pemberley and suddenly have an image of her. It had been impossible to forget her.

But that did not mean he wanted to meet her again. And, if he met her again, he was not sure how to react, which was an unusual feeling for him because he was usually very decisive. If he acknowledged Miss Elizabeth – always assuming it was the same family – then he would, in effect, be encouraging her, and he was still of the opinion that she was not good enough to be a friend for his sister.

And yet his sister had not shown any great affection for the other women he had put in her way. They had not been able to help her to recover from her abduction, and small wonder, as they did not know about it.

But Miss Elizabeth knew.

He wondered if she would have gossiped about it. If so, he would soon know, because he would hear mention of it. If not . . . well, if she could be discreet, perhaps she was not so unsuitable after all.

He glanced across at his sister. He loved her deeply, even though he was not a man who showed his emotions, and in that moment his decision was made. He would do anything to help her, and if that meant being polite to Miss Elizabeth Bennet, then he would do it.

He gave a soft, inward smile. Despite his pride and his arrogant nature, he found himself hoping it was the same Bennets, and that before long, he would see the impertinent, courageous and thoroughly exasperating Miss Elizabeth Bennet again.

Chapter Six

The night of the Meryton assembly arrived. Mr Darcy was ready early and passed the remaining half hour before the carriage was brought round by playing at chess with his sister. She was very quiet and twice he had to remind her that it was her move. She was too young to attend the assembly, being only fifteen and not yet out, but she would have company this evening because Louisa Hurst had offered to remain behind with her. Mr Hurst had offered to stay behind, too. He was a lazy man, and he did not like to make any effort, so staying at home suited him.

Caroline Bingley had arranged a great many activities for Georgiana's entertainment, but had not offered to stay behind herself. The reason for that was clear. She had set her cap at Mr Darcy and did not want to be parted from him, especially at an assembly ball where she knew he would dance with her. He did not like to dance with strangers and so she was sure of having him as a partner.

At last it was time for them to leave. The carriage drove through pretty country lanes, which were silvered under dappled moonlight, and finally it arrived at the assembly rooms.

Mr Darcy suppressed a feeling of distaste as he stepped out of the carriage. The building was small and the rooms would be also be small and cramped.

'I know just how you feel,' said Caroline Bingley. 'The paltriness of the establishment cannot be expected to delight your fastidious tastes.'

She picked up the hem of her skirt and wrinkled her nose as she walked inside.

Mr Darcy had been feeling the same, but he did not want to agree with Miss Bingley and so he said, 'It is well enough.'

'I think it is positively delightful!' said Mr Bingley with a wide smile.

He was a good natured man and he was of a cheerful disposition, which was why Mr Darcy liked him. He looked at the world with a view to finding it delightful and so he was always pleased with what he saw. As they went in, everything met with his approval. The rooms, the people – all brought compliments from him.

But Mr Darcy thought the room even worse than he had imagined. Its ceiling was low and there was scarcely a chandelier in sight. The people were dressed in homely clothes that were several years behind the London fashions. There was no elegance in their movements and their voices sounded uncultured to his ears.

His gaze travelled round the room and then fell on a face he recognised. Miss Elizabeth Bennet was standing at the opposite side of the room. Even in the dim candlelight there was no mistaking her. But had she said anything about his sister's ordeal?

As he heard the wave of whispers running round the room, he realised she had kept Georgiana's secret, for the whispers talked only of his wealth and his country estate. There was not one whisper about his sister.

He felt a sense of gratitude and admiration for her. He knew that people loved to gossip, but Miss Elizabeth had refrained from saying anything, even though she had a particularly juicy piece of gossip at her disposal, and so Georgiana's reputation was safe.

His friend, Mr Bingley, quickly found the prettiest young lady in the room and started to dance with her, while Caroline Bingley stood at the side of the room with Mr Darcy.

'These people!' she said. 'How clumsy they are! Without style or beauty!'

For the most part, Mr Darcy privately agreed, but the more he looked at Miss Elizabeth, the more he thought her face improved on acquaintance. She was not beautiful in the common way, but there was a strength in her countenance and an openness in her expression which he found pleasing.

He had an opportunity to study her more closely a few minutes later when one of her friends took her arm in a sisterly way and led her across the room. As he saw her walking past him he could not help noticing her eyes, which were just as fine as he remembered.

The dance came to an end and Mr Bingley approached him.

'Is it not wonderful?' asked Mr Bingley. 'I have never met with pleasanter people or prettier girls in all my life. Everybody has been most kind and attentive. There is no formality, no stiffness. I feel at home already. And as to Miss Bennet —'

Ah! thought Mr Darcy. *So Bingley's partner is Miss Elizabeth's' sister.*

' — I cannot conceive of an angel more beautiful. Come, Darcy, I must have you dance. One of Miss Bennet's sisters is sitting down just behind you, who is very pretty and I dare say very agreeable. Do let me ask my partner to introduce you.'

The words were music to Mr Darcy's ears. Here was a way for him to be introduced to Miss Elizabeth formally, without him having to ask for the introduction.

'Thank you, Bingley. I will.'

'Capital!' said Mr Bingley with a happy smile. 'I will ask Miss Bennet to bring her sister over to us and make the introductions.'

Elizabeth was deliberately ignoring Mr Darcy. She had been shocked when she had first seen him and she had let out a startled exclamation, but someone had trodden on the hem of her white muslin gown at that moment, and so the exclamation had passed off. After her first surprise, she had turned away from him. He had made it clear he did not wish to continue the acquaintance and she had no intention of forcing herself on his notice.

Luckily, something much more pleasant soon occurred: Mr Bingley asked Jane to dance. Ever since Mr Bingley had paid a call on their father, soon after his arrival at Netherfield Park, Elizabeth had been aware that Jane admired him. The young ladies had not spoken to him on that occasion, but they had seen him from an upstairs window and he had looked very agreeable. Jane had remarked on his pleasant countenance and his restrained clothes, which had been fashionable without being ostentatious, for he had worn a pair of cream pantaloons and a blue coat. She had mentioned him once or twice since, which was unusual, since Jane – unlike Lydia! – rarely talked about young men.

But when they arrived at the assembly, Elizabeth noticed that her sister's gaze wandered round the room, and she saw her sister blush at the sight of Mr Bingley. So Elizabeth was very pleased when he asked her sister to dance.

And now the dance was over and Jane was coming towards her.

Elizabeth was disappointed that Jane was no longer dancing, but all the same she was glad to have someone to confide in, for Mr Darcy's entrance had been a decided shock.

'Elizabeth! It is so wonderful! I have been dancing with Mr Bingley and he is quite the most agreeable gentleman imaginable,' said Jane shyly. 'And now he has asked me to introduce you to his friend.'

She turned and looked over her shoulder, to where Mr Bingley was standing with Mr Darcy.

'Oh, no!' said Elizabeth.

Jane looked surprised.

'Jane, his friend is Mr Darcy!'

'Mr Darcy?' Jane's eyes went wide with surprise. 'You don't mean he is the man you met in Ramsgate?'

'The very same. I was never more surprised in my life than when I saw him enter the room. I cannot dance with him,' said Elizabeth. 'He will look down his nose at me and make me uncomfortable. I am surprised he consented to attend a country assembly in the first place.'

'He does look rather out of place,' Jane admitted.

His black coat was made of a far finer grade of wool than the other coats in the room, and his cream pantaloons were made of a far superior material, too. They fit his powerful legs without wrinkling, pulling firmly across his thighs. His hair was combed into a fashionable Brutus style and his dark eyes were full of pride. His high cheekbones and firm jaw were a marked contrast to the more homely features around him. He surveyed the room as a king would survey a country tavern and he looked as if it were a punishment for him to be there.

'Then what am I to tell him?' asked Jane. 'Am I to say that you will not dance with him?'

Elizabeth was tempted to say, "Yes, tell him exactly that". But to do so would be rude, and just because Mr Darcy was rude did not mean that she had to behave in the same way. And so she said, 'Of course not. You must introduce me. I dare say it will not be so bad.'

'Thank you, Lizzy!' said Jane.

Her words were heartfelt, for she liked Mr Bingley very much and Elizabeth guessed at once that she did not want to insult his friend.

Jane led Elizabeth across the room and made the introductions. Elizabeth dropped a curtsey, her long white gown sweeping beneath her as she did so.

Mr Darcy bowed.

The next dance was about to begin. Mr Bingley escorted Jane to their place in the set, and Mr Darcy escorted Elizabeth.

Everyone turned to look and a whisper of '. . . lucky Miss Bennets . . .' reached her ears.

But Elizabeth did not feel lucky. Although any other young lady in the room would have gladly swapped places with her, Elizabeth knew that Mr Darcy had a great many faults and that his fortune did not make up for them.

'You are surprised to find me here,' he said, as the dance began.

'I am indeed,' she said.

'It was quite by chance. My friend, Mr Bingley, rented Netherfield Park and invited me to stay. I did not know it was in your neighbourhood, or else —'

'You would not have come?' Elizabeth enquired.

He shook his head. 'You misunderstand me. It is quite the contrary.'

'Oh?' Elizabeth's eyebrows raised in astonishment.

'Yes, I am relieved to be here and now that I am here I realise I should have come sooner. You see, Miss Elizabeth, my sister has been very unhappy for the last few weeks. I hoped that, once we returned to Pemberley, she would regain her spirits, but it did not happen. The physician recommended a change of scene, and so when Mr Bingley rented Netherfield Park I was glad to bring her here for a visit. But even the new scene did not lift her spirits.'

'I did warn you that she needed young women of her own age to talk to,' said Elizabeth.

'And I listened to you.'

Her eyebrows shot up still further.

'Mr Darcy, you amaze me!' she said.

He gave a rare smile, and she thought how attractive it made him look. His gaze softened and Elizabeth noticed how handsome his eyes were. They were deep set and a velvety brown. When they were not lit up by arrogance they were surprisingly warm, and a strong intelligence lurked there.

'I am glad that I am not predictable,' he said.

Elizabeth was forced to smile.

The steps of the dance parted them and by the time they came back together he said, 'But despite finding her other young women to talk to, she is still listless.'

'Forgive me, Mr Darcy, but by "young women" do you mean Mr Bingley's sisters? For they are older than I am, and consequently much older than your sister.'

He looked surprised.

'They are still of an age with her.'

'I think not,' said Elizabeth. 'Georgiana is of an age with my sister, Lydia.'

As soon as she said it, she wished it unsaid, for Lydia was laughing loudly at the other end of the room and dancing with wild abandon.

Mr Darcy followed her gaze and looked astonished, then haughty. It was obvious he had no wish for his sister to behave in such a wild manner. Although, remembering Georgiana's pale, sad face, Elizabeth thought that it would be no bad thing if Georgiana could acquire a little of Lydia's spirit.

'Perhaps you are right,' he said. 'But it has occurred to me that she needs someone to confide in, and as you are the only person who knows of her predicament, I wonder if I might persuade you to call on her tomorrow? If you would befriend her, I think it might do much to ease her spirit. Her face lit up when she heard mention of your name and it is the first time I have seen any life in her since Ramsgate.'

Elizabeth shook her head.

'I do not think that will be possible,' she said.

His face fell.

'Then you still bear me a grudge for the way I spoke to you in Ramsgate,' he said in a chagrined tone of voice. 'I am a proud man, Miss Elizabeth, but, for my sister's sake I am willing to humble myself and beg your forgiveness.'

'You misunderstand me,' she hastened to reassure him. 'I was going to say, it will not be possible as we are engaged elsewhere, but I would be glad to see your sister the day after tomorrow.'

His brow darkened.

'So I have humbled myself for nothing,' he said, clearly wishing it undone. 'You were agreeable to my suggestion anyway.'

'If you see it as humbling yourself to apologise, then yes,' said Elizabeth. 'If you see it as a normal part of life, then no.'

His eyes widened in surprise, then he said, 'You have an unusual way of looking at the world.'

'No,' she said with an arch smile,' it is you who have an unusual way of looking at the world, Mr Darcy. No one else would think twice before apologising if they were in the wrong. And you were in the wrong, you know. I do not think less of you for doing it, in fact I think more of you, particularly as you did it to help your sister. I would do anything to help mine.'

Mr Darcy glanced at Jane.

'She is a very beautiful young woman.'

'She is, inside and out,' said Elizabeth. The steps of the dance parted them again. When they met once more, she continued, 'I think it would do your sister good to meet mine. Jane's calm goodness always makes me feel better, just by being with her, and I think it would make Georgiana feel the same. I will bring her with me when I call.'

'Two sisters. It would remind her of —'

The final chord of the dance sounded and Elizabeth was disappointed, for Mr Darcy's words had aroused her interest and she thought he had been about to say something important. But there was no help for it, the dance had ended, and so she curtseyed and Mr Darcy bowed.

'I say,' said Mr Bingley, coming up to them with Jane. 'Was that not splendid, Darcy? I cannot think when I have ever enjoyed myself more.'

Mr Bingley had now danced twice with Jane and could not dance with her a third time, for such a thing was never done.

Elizabeth wondered if Mr Darcy would ask

her for another dance, but evidently he did not feel he could say anything further to her in a crowded ballroom.

He made her a bow and walked away.

It would remind her of . . . thought Elizabeth, recalling his enigmatic words.

What had Mr Darcy been about to say?

Chapter Seven

Elizabeth and Jane had much to talk over that night as they undressed for bed.

'You seemed to enjoy yourself very much tonight,' said Elizabeth.

'Oh, Lizzy, is not Mr Bingley the most agreeable man you have ever met?' asked Jane, her eyes shining.

'I do not know, since I did not have a chance to say more than a few words to him. He was too busy dancing with you, or fetching you an ice, or talking to you!' Elizabeth teased her.

'Oh, Lizzy, for shame! We did not spend any more time together than was proper.'

'But no less time, either.'

'We seemed to have so much to say to each other. Never has someone else's character chimed so perfectly with my own.'

'You deserve all the happiness life has to offer,' said Elizabeth. 'I am very happy for you.'

'Lizzy, what do you mean?' asked Jane with a blush.

'That he is falling in love with you,' said Elizabeth.

'You go too fast!' Jane protested. 'We have only just met.'

'But time has very little to do with it,' said Elizabeth. 'It is possible to know a man for years and not have anything to say to him. Equally, it is possible to know a man for a very short space of time and be intrigued by him.'

As she spoke, she was not thinking of Mr Bingley, but of Mr Darcy.

She had been shocked to see him at the assembly . . . and then just as shocked to find that he was capable of being polite.

Despite her bad first impression of him, she had to admit that he could be agreeable if he chose, and his devotion to his sister won her respect. She loved her own sister dearly, and so she could understand his feelings in that matter.

'I have promised we will call at Netherfield the day after tomorrow,' said Elizabeth.

She told Jane everything Mr Darcy had said.

'It reflects well on him,' said Jane. 'And I am sure I am willing to help his sister. She must feel very alone, with no mother or sisters to talk to.'

'We will soon have her feeling more cheerful,' said Elizabeth. 'We must invite her here often. Perhaps some of Lydia's high spirits will rub off on her!'

Jane gave a shudder. 'Oh, not too much, I hope. I love our sister dearly, but there is no escaping the fact that she can be very embarrassing at times. She was laughing so loudly tonight, it drew attention, and Mr Bingley said he wondered that her parents did not do something about it. That was before he knew she was my sister, whereupon he apologised and said he liked to see young ladies enjoying themselves.'

'I fear Lydia will never be made to behave. Mama encourages her, and Papa —'

She did not need to say any more. Elizabeth loved her father dearly, but he was lazy where his daughters were concerned, and he did not seek to correct them. He allowed Mary to continue on her own pompous way, and he did not try to curb Kitty's frivolousness. Nor did he do anything to stop Lydia's wild behaviour.

'Never mind,' said Elizabeth. 'It would be too much to hope for, that I should have four sisters like you, Jane. I am just glad that I have one!'

She gave her sister a hug and jumped into bed.

Jane climbed into bed more slowly.

'Still thinking of Mr Bingley?' Elizabeth teased her.

Jane blushed.

'Oh, Lizzy, I know it is foolish of me to like him so well, so quickly, but I cannot help thinking that he is everything I want in a young man.'

'Then I am very pleased he moved into the neighbourhood,' said Elizabeth.

'And Mr Darcy?' asked Jane. 'Are you pleased he is here?'

Elizabeth's brow darkened. As she blew out the candle she said, 'That remains to be seen.'

*

Two days later, the ladies of Longbourn waited on the ladies of Netherfield Park. Mrs Bennet chaperoned her daughters to Netherfield and did everything in her power to further an attachment between Mr Bingley and Jane.

Elizabeth felt sorry for her sister. Mrs Bennet's behaviour was very obvious and it was embarrassing. But Mr Bingley did not seem to mind. Indeed, he did not seem to notice. He was too busy looking at Jane.

Mr Bingley's sisters noticed, however, and exchanged mocking glances.

Elizabeth blushed for her mother, but Mrs Bennet carried on singing Jane's praises in a most obvious manner.

The one good thing about it was that it meant Elizabeth had a chance to speak to Georgiana without interruption, and when Georgiana invited Elizabeth to take a turn about the gardens, Mr Darcy said he would escort them. He then turned to Kitty and made a point of inviting her, too.

Luckily, Mary and Lydia were over by the pianoforte, Mary playing and Lydia laughing at her, so they did not ask to come along. Mr Bingley's sisters were talking to Jane, and by the time Caroline Bingley realised what was afoot, it was too late for her to join Mr Darcy's party as they were already halfway out of the room.

They walked through the magnificent hall,

with its marble pillars and its black and white floor, and out of the imposing front door. The autumn sunshine fell on their faces and made it a pleasure to be out of doors. The gardens were looking very pretty. The bright colours of the summer flowers had given way to the darker oranges and golds of autumn, which were set off by the lush green foliage. Gravel paths ran through the gardens, leading across the lawns to fountains and avenues and smaller enclosed gardens.

'It was a good idea to invite Kitty,' said Elizabeth, as her small party walked along the paths, with the gravel crunching beneath their feet.

She and Mr Darcy were a little ahead of the two young girls, who were walking more slowly.

'Yes. She is less wild than your other sister, and she is of an age with Georgiana. I hope the two of them will get on well together - you see, I have attended to you,' said Mr Darcy with a bow.

'Yes, you have,' Elizabeth acknowledged.

There was something of a breeze, which was tugging at her bonnet, and so Elizabeth steered their steps to the rose garden. She had known Netherfield Park all her life and she knew the rose garden was enclosed and therefore sheltered.

They went through a pretty door in a high

wall and the wind instantly dropped. Ahead of them were many flower beds where the roses still bloomed despite the lateness of the year. The walls held the heat and the lovely flowers perfumed the air with their sweet scent. Georgiana and Kitty went over to the blooms and buried their noses in them, then decided to collect the fallen petals to make scent.

Mr Darcy stood and watched his sister enjoying herself with Kitty as the two young ladies collected handfuls of pink petals.

'I have not seen Georgiana looking so happy for a long time,' he said.

Elizabeth watched the two young ladies with pleasure.

'I think she and Georgiana will become friends,' she said. 'They will do each other good. Kitty will lift Georgiana's spirits and Georgiana will have a calming influence on Kitty. Kitty has not had any suitable friends of her own age, either. Lydia is too wild and Mary is too dour. She and Georgiana can talk about all the things that interest girls of their age. They can stroll in the gardens and make flower collections and *pot pourris* and other such things when the weather is good, and they can look through fashion books together and read novels together when it rains.'

'Novels?' asked Mr Darcy with a frown. 'I am not sure that novels are suitable reading for Georgiana.'

'On the contrary, they will lift her spirits,' said Elizabeth, turning towards him with confidence. 'That is what you want, is it not?'

Mr Darcy reluctantly agreed. 'Yes, it is,' he said. 'Perhaps one or two novels, carefully chosen, would not be so terrible.'

Elizabeth knew it was not easy for him to change and she gave him full credit for being prepared to do so. She could not expect him to do so all at once, but he had made a start.

'I must thank you for not betraying my sister's confidence,' he said, turning to Elizabeth and looking at her sincerely.

'Did you think I would?' asked Elizabeth in surprise.

Mr Darcy pursed his lips. 'I have few illusions where life is concerned,' he said. 'There are very few people who can keep a confidence, even if they swear to do so, and you have no reason to keep this one. Georgiana was not a member of your family, and I —'

'Yes?' Elizabeth prompted him.

'I had not been very polite to you,' he said.

'Not very polite?' Elizabeth laughed. 'Mr Darcy, you had been extremely rude!'

He looked ashamed of himself. 'Yes, I had. It was not well done of me. But I did not know you then and I had no reason to trust you. Even so, you kept Georgiana's confidence, and I know how much ladies like to gossip,' he said.

'I cannot pretend to be better than the rest of

my sex where that is concerned,' said Elizabeth, 'but I hope I know the difference between harmless gossip and the kind of gossip that will cause a great deal of unhappiness. Your sister's secret is safe with me.'

'I know it and I thank you for it. My sister is very precious to me and it is both my duty and my privilege to care for her.'

The two young ladies had by this time gathered the fallen rose petals and wrapped them in their handkerchiefs. Elizabeth suggested they should leave the rose garden and go down the long walk to the folly, and they all agreed. It was in a sheltered avenue and they would be out of the wind.

Georgiana and Kitty walked ahead, chattering happily.

As she saw Mr Darcy's eyes lingering on his sister, Elizabeth said, 'Sometimes there can be too much care. Forgive me for speaking frankly, but you watch over her with more attention than is needed.'

'Since the business with Mr Wickham, can you blame me?' he asked.

'Perhaps not, but you have always done so, have you not? I had an opportunity to talk to Georgiana when we were in Ramsgate, and I understand that she did not go to school.'

'No, she did not. But neither did you.'

Elizabeth looked surprised that he should know this, but he said, 'Georgiana mentioned it.'

'Ah.' Elizabeth nodded, understanding.

She continued to walk down the long, gravel path to the folly which stood at the end of it. It was a small building with open sides supported by columns and a domed roof. When they reached it, Elizabeth and Darcy sat on the seat that ran round the inside, while Georgiana and Kitty amused themselves by arranging their rose petals on the grass, according to size.

'It is true, I did not go to school,' said Elizabeth, turning to look at him. 'But I had four sisters to play with, and talk to, and walk with. Your sister has no one.'

'Perhaps you are right. But, you see, since our father's death – our mother died when Georgiana was very young – I have had to be both parents to Georgiana as well as a brother.'

Elizabeth thought how hard that must have been for him. Her parents were decidedly odd, for she had a silly and embarrassing mother, and a lazy father, but even so they were her parents and she loved them. There would have been a big hole in her life if they had died, and she was full of sympathy as she realised that, for Mr Darcy, that hole in his life was real and he had to live with it day by day. So did his sister. Small wonder, then, that he tried to fill that hole for her by being father, mother and brother all at once.

'I understand,' she said, and her voice showed that she did, truly, understand. 'Even so, many parents send their children to school,' she continued. 'If you were being parents to her as well as a brother, could you not have found some good school for her, so that she could make friends?'

He winced.

She was surprised at his extreme reaction. She knew that he thought highly of himself and the Darcy name but this was taking things too far.

'Many girls from the best families go to select seminaries,' she continued. 'Surely even a man as proud as you are must know of some school you would find suitable for your sister?'

'No!' he said, jumping up and striding around the folly.

She was astonished at his vehemence.

'Are the Darcys really so high they cannot mix with anyone else?' she asked, her eyes wide open and her eyebrows raised.

He gave a shuddering sigh and sat down again. He leant forward, and for a moment she thought he was going to put his head in his hands, but instead he rested his elbows on his knees. Then, having collected himself, he sat back again.

'You misunderstand me,' he said, shaking his head.

He turned to look at her and she could tell he was undecided about something. Then he gave an almost invisible nod of his head, as if to himself, as he made his decision.

'It is not my custom to speak openly to people,' he began, 'but something about your own openness and trustworthiness has unlocked something inside me and I find myself willing to speak to you.'

Elizabeth waited with bated breath, wondering what was coming.

'You have perhaps noticed there is a wide gap in ages between my sister and myself,' he went on. 'I am twenty-eight years old and my sister is fifteen.'

He glanced towards Georgiana, who was still busily occupied in playing with her rose petals. Her laughter, accompanied by Kitty's laughter, reached them through the crisp autumn air.

'I had not thought of it, but yes,' said Elizabeth.

'There was not always such a large gap. We had two sisters. Catherine, named after my aunt, Lady Catherine de Bourgh, and Anne, named after my mother, came in between us. They were both sent away to school, a very good establishment, from the age of eleven. But there was an epidemic at the school. My sisters were both there at the time. The school acted responsibly and called the best doctors but it made no difference. Catherine was one of the first to catch the fever and she died very quickly. Anne died a week later. It threw Pemberley into a terrible period of mourning. My mother never recovered from the shock. She had not been in good health since the birth of Georgiana, and she faded rapidly after the deaths of my sisters. Less than six months later, she followed them to the grave.'

Elizabeth felt tears gathering on her eyelashes and she felt a sob rising in her throat. She listened in silence to his speech because she knew what it cost him to make it but she longed to reach out and comfort him, and she would have done so, if it had been permissible. His tension, his horror, his fear and his distress were etched on his face as he relived the memories and Elizabeth's heart turned over inside her chest. He had known so much loss and borne it so bravely . . . She felt humbled that he had chosen to share such intimate memories with her.

'Mr Darcy, I am so sorry,' she said.

There was a catch in her throat and she did not dare say more, for fear of crying.

'I have upset you. That was not my intention,' he said, turning towards her with eyes full of concern.

And what eyes they were. They were warm, soft and velvety, and they, too, swam with tears. She had never seen his eyes look like that before. They were usually hard and arrogant, but she saw now that his pride was a shield, something to protect him from further loss and suffering and to hold the pain at bay. Again, she wanted to reach out and touch him but such things were forbidden.

'It is no matter,' she said, taking her handkerchief out of her reticule. 'It is nothing next to your suffering. I think that you, as well as your sister, have not had anyone to talk to for a very long time.'

He nodded in acknowledgement of the sympathy in her voice and she knew he was grateful for it. It had created a bond between them that would be hard to break.

'I do not know what came over me,' he said as he blinked the tears away. 'I should not have mentioned it. An English gentlemen does not talk of such things. He does not reveal his feelings. Forgive me.'

'There is nothing to forgive,' she said, looking at him with bright eyes, her head held high. 'I feel privileged that you have confided in me.' She added, 'I need hardly say that your confidence is safe with me.'

'Yes. I know it is,' he said softly.

He laid his hand on top of hers and Elizabeth felt a touching of their hearts and souls. It was the most powerful thing she had ever felt.

'Miss Elizabeth —' he began.

The moment was broken by Mrs Bennet's loud voice calling, 'We have come to join you. Such a beautiful day! Mr Bingley was wild to show Jane the garden.'

Elizabeth felt that her mother's intrusion

could not have been worse timed. Mr Darcy withdrew his hand and stood up. But something of their closeness lingered. It was in the air, even though they were no longer touching, and she still felt connected to him.

She took a few moments to gather her thoughts. She dabbed her eyes and returned her handkerchief to her reticule. Then she walked out of the folly and went towards her mother's party, who were approaching down the gravel walk.

Mr Bingley was looking embarrassed, as well he might, for of course he had not been "wild to show Jane the garden". Elizabeth doubted if Mr Bingley could ever be wild about anything! But he certainly looked pleased to be with Jane, and proud to be escorting her round his grounds.

Mr Darcy followed Elizabeth out of the folly at a discreet distance.

Caroline Bingley did not look pleased, in fact she looked as if she were angry, and only containing her anger with the greatest difficulty. The reason was not difficult to discover. She admired Mr Darcy greatly, and she wanted to be Mrs Darcy, and so the fact that he had chosen to escort Elizabeth around the gardens had seriously annoyed her.

Georgiana and Kitty picked up their rose petals and the whole party gathered together out in the autumn sunshine.

Elizabeth felt a sense of loss and growing

exasperation. Not only had she lost the chance for any further intimate discussions with Mr Darcy, but her family was behaving in the most embarrassing way.

Lydia had claimed Georgiana's arm and was laughing in an immoderate fashion. Mrs Bennet was talking very loudly about a young man who had written Jane a poem. Mary was saying that the poem had been badly written, and that the young man should have studied Milton in order to write something of worth. In fact, Elizabeth thought her family could not have embarrassed her more if they had set out with that express intention.

Miss Bingley, meanwhile, was delighted that Elizabeth's family were behaving in such a ridiculous fashion. She looked more and more pleased with every shout from Lydia, and every ridiculous remark from Mrs Bennet. It was not hard to see why. With every shameful comment from Elizabeth's family, Miss Bingley felt her own chances of securing Mr Darcy increasing, and she made several genteel comments, as if to point up the very great difference between the vulgar Bennets and her own refined behaviour.

Elizabeth was not worried, however, for she knew that Mr Darcy had no liking for Miss Bingley.

Even so, she wished her family was not quite so embarrassing.

She and Jane exchanged resigned glances.

They were both of them being let down by their relations.

Elizabeth glanced at Mr Bingley. The poor man did not know how to reply to Mrs Bennet's silly comments. If he was still eager to see Jane after this, he must be falling in love! thought Elizabeth.

And what of Mr Darcy? She glanced towards him. He held himself aloof, a little apart from the others, as if he were still recovering from the powerful memories he had just experienced. He had confided in her in a way she suspected he had never confided in anyone before and she was deeply touched.

He appeared cold and arrogant on the surface, and yet beneath that surface there beat the heart of a caring and loving man. She felt that such a combination was capable of shattering her calm existence and throwing her into all the turmoil of falling in love.

But did Mr Darcy really want to shatter her calm?

And was she ready to let him?

Chapter Eight

The ladies of Netherfield returned the call a few days later. Mr Bingley and Mr Darcy escorted them.

Mrs Bennet was nearly frantic as she saw them approaching the house.

'Hill! Hill! We have visitors! Oh, the house is so untidy! Lydia, why must you leave your bonnets lying about in such a manner?'

'Because I am trimming them,' said Lydia.

'And Kitty! Why must you cough so?' demanded Mrs Bennet.

'I am sure I don't mean to cough,' said Kitty, who was understandably put out.

'Mary, stop that caterwauling and help me to tidy the room!' said Mrs Bennet, bundling a pile of mending into Mary's arms. 'Now take that to the laundry room. And Jane! Jane, go and change your gown. Mr Bingley has seen you in that one. Put on your lemon muslin. Oh, Elizabeth! You had better change your gown, too. Mr Darcy seems to have taken a fancy to you and you should encourage him. He is very wealthy and he has a huge estate in Derbyshire. Only marry him, and we will all be settled for life!'

Elizabeth went upstairs and together she and Jane changed their gowns. By the time they returned to the drawing-room, the Netherfield party was at the front door. A minute later, they were shown into the drawing-room.

There was the usual bowing and curtseying as greetings were exchanged.

Elizabeth was pleased to see that Georgiana had more colour than she had done at their last meeting. She appeared more animated and was able to smile and answer politely when Mrs Bennet enquired after her health.

They talked of the weather, of the garden, of the Bingleys' carriage and half a dozen other such topics before Mrs Bennet said, 'Jane, I am sure Mr Bingley would like to see our wilderness garden.' She turned to Mr Bingley. 'It is not so grand as the Netherfield wilderness, but it is thought very pretty all the same.'

'I should like to see it very much,' said Mr Bingley, jumping up.

'Would you care to see it, Miss Darcy?' asked Elizabeth.

'Oh, yes, thank you, I would,' said Georgiana.

Mr Darcy did not offer to escort them and Elizabeth understood why. Miss Bingley did not like to let him out of her sight, and she would have demanded to go too if Mr Darcy had been one of the party. They had been lucky to escape her before but they could not count on having such luck again. And if Miss Bingley accompanied them, it would prevent Elizabeth having any private talk with Georgiana. So Mr Darcy had obviously decided to stay in the drawing-room and endure the silliness of Mrs Bennet, and the possessiveness of Caroline Bingley, so that his sister could unburden herself.

Elizabeth honoured him for it.

After donning their outdoor things, Mr Bingley offered Jane his arm and then, followed by Elizabeth and Georgiana, went outside.

Jane and Mr Bingley soon fell behind as Elizabeth and Georgiana bent their steps towards the wilderness garden. The orange and gold leaves swished beneath their feet as they did so.

'What a change in the weather,' said Georgiana. 'When you came to Netherfield, the day was warm despite the wind, but now there is the nip of autumn in the air. There are falling leaves everywhere.'

She was right. Even now they were swirling down from the trees, like slow birds gliding down to the ground.

'Yes, indeed,' said Elizabeth, drawing her cloak around her. 'We did not have a chance for truly private conversation at Netherfield, but I hope you know you can confide in me at any time,' she continued. 'Your brother is worried about you. He thinks you have not recovered from your shock.'

'Dear Fitzwilliam, he is always so careful of

me.'

Elizabeth thought about what he had told her, that he had lost two sisters in an epidemic, and her heart went out to him again. It also went out to Georgiana, who must barely be able to remember her sisters.

'And have you recovered from your shock?' asked Elizabeth kindly.

'A week ago, I would have said no,' said Georgiana. 'But now I am starting to feel the shadow lifting. I could not talk to anyone about it, you see, and I felt I had to be watchful in case I let anything slip by mistake. But now I know I can talk about it whenever I wish – thanks to you, Elizabeth – I feel the burden has gone from me. It is true that Mr Wickham hurt me very much, and his behaviour shocked me, and I should like to talk about it, if you do not mind.'

'I would welcome it, if it will put your mind at ease,' said Elizabeth.

'You see, I meet so few people, and I do not know how people in the wider world behave. I cannot help thinking that I must have been to blame. I keep asking myself if I was too friendly to Mr Wickham. Did I encourage him?'

'You did not,' said Elizabeth robustly.

'But I was very friendly towards him. He was not to blame for thinking that I would welcome his advances.'

'Of course he was. He knew very well that what you felt for him was friendship, occasioned by growing up on the same estate. He deliberately set out to ensnare you because he wanted your fortune, and he was entirely to blame for abducting you when you refused to go with him willingly. If he had had any proper interest in you, he would have asked your brother if he could court you, so you must not blame yourself for anything. Nothing was your fault.'

'Oh, thank you! You set my mind at rest. I have had no one to ask, you see. I could not ask Mrs Annesley because she does not know what happened in Ramsgate and I could not possibly tell her. I have been very worried about it.'

'That is a terrible burden to bear alone for so many months. No wonder your spirits were low. But now you do not have to worry about it any more.'

Georgiana took her hand impulsively and squeezed it.

Elizabeth returned the pressure.

'You are lucky to have so many sisters,' said Georgiana. 'You always have someone to talk to. I think you are very close to Jane.'

'Yes, I am,' said Elizabeth. She went on gently, 'Your brother told me that you, too, had sisters, but that they died. I am sorry.'

Georgiana was surprised.

'My brother has never spoken of it to anyone outside the family before. He must like you very much.'

The artless sentence, so simply uttered, touched Elizabeth deeply. She found herself increasingly drawn to the proud man who seemed so harsh on the surface but who was quite otherwise underneath.

'I think you like my sister, Kitty?' asked Elizabeth, as they entered the wilderness garden.

'Yes,' said Georgiana. 'We both like blue ribbons and dislike yellow. We prefer silk to satin, and we prefer muslin to sarsenet.' She blushed. 'I dare say such things seem trivial to you, but I have never had anyone to share such things with. My conversations at home revolve around art and music. They have to be educational, you see.'

Elizabeth laughed. 'You do not need to worry about having an educational conversation with Kitty! She has no interest in anything educational. I think she is doing you good. I think you will do her good, too. She spends too much time with Lydia, and my youngest sister is inclined to be silly. Your influence will show her that it is possible to be more elegant and still have fun.'

'I admire Lydia's spirits,' said Georgiana. 'But she is just a little wild.'

'You are too kind!' said Elizabeth. 'Lydia is *very* wild!'

They had by now walked through the wilderness and they set off back towards the house.

As they approached the door, they stopped and waited for Mr Bingley and Jane to join them.

'Mr Bingley is very taken with your sister,' said Georgiana.

'Yes, he is.'

'Does she like him, too? I cannot make her out. She is so serene that I have difficulty knowing what her feelings are.'

'In confidence, she likes him very much,' said Elizabeth.

'I am glad. I think my brother would like me to marry Mr Bingley when I am older, but although I like him, I could not think of him as a husband.'

'Then tell your brother so. He will listen to you now, I think.'

'Oh, I could not say such a thing to him!' said Georgiana in consternation.

'My dear Georgiana, life will be so much easier for you and your brother if you learn to talk to each other, believe me.'

'Perhaps you are right,' said Georgiana. 'I will try.'

Jane and Mr Bingley drew level with them and they all went into the house.

Once they had removed their outdoor clothes they returned to the drawing-room. Mr Darcy had a pained expression on his face and Elizabeth felt sorry for him. He had been trapped with Mrs Bennet for half an hour, and that was not a fate she would wish on anyone!

The Netherfield party soon took their leave, but not before inviting Jane, Kitty and Elizabeth to dine with them in a few days' time.

'The gentlemen will be dining with the officers,' said Miss Bingley, 'and we will be short of company.'

It was hardly the most polite way of phrasing the invitation, but Elizabeth did not much care. She knew that she, Jane and Kitty could raise Georgiana's spirits still further, and she was glad of an opportunity of doing so.

She was also glad of an opportunity to see Mr Darcy again, as well, for although he would be dining with the officers, she would be likely to see him at some point.

She could not help wondering what he had been about to say to her at Netherfield Park, when they had been so rudely interrupted by Mrs Bennet.

Chapter Nine

Elizabeth chose a simple sprigged muslin gown for dinner at Netherfield Park. She could not compete with Miss Bingley and Mrs Hurst in terms of dress, for they were both very fine ladies and wore silk and satin even in the daytime. Such rich fabrics were quite beyond Elizabeth's means, for although her family's income was adequate, it did not stretch to such luxuries. There were five Miss Bennets to clothe, and so they had to be content with sarsenet and muslin. But Elizabeth did not mind. The sprigged muslin suited her, and its simplicity suited her open temperament.

Jane chose a white sarsenet gown, which made her look like a beautiful Grecian statue, for she was tall and elegant, and Kitty chose a spotted muslin.

'Why wasn't I invited?' demanded Lydia. 'I am sure I am more interesting than Kitty. Miss Bingley should have invited me.'

'When you have learned to behave like a young lady, perhaps you will be invited to sensible gatherings,' said Mary. 'Join me in a reading of Fordyce's sermons, Lydia. They will teach you how to go on.'

Lydia rolled her eyes then gave a heavy sigh and threw herself onto the sofa.

When the three young ladies were ready, Jane asked if they could have the carriage to take them to Netherfield.

'I suppose you must,' said Mrs Bennet, in an aggrieved tone of voice. 'If you had been invited on your own, Jane, I would have sent you on horseback, so that if it started to rain Miss Bingley would have to invite you to stay the night. But as there are three of you, you will have to take the carriage.'

The carriage was duly organised and the three young ladies set out.

Their mother's hopes for rain were realised, but inside the carriage they remained dry.

'What a good thing we had the carriage,' said Kitty. 'Our hair and clothes would have been ruined otherwise.'

They soon arrived at Netherfield Park, where they were made welcome in accordance with the characters of the different ladies. Miss Bingley gave Elizabeth and Kitty a supercilious nod, but was a little more friendly to Jane. Mrs Hurst declared it was prodigiously good of them to call, and confessed she would have been bored to death without them. Georgiana was warm and friendly, greeting them all with genuine affection.

Elizabeth was pleased to see how well Georgiana and Kitty got on. They were soon examining a book of fashion plates and exclaiming over the latest styles of gowns and bonnets.

Miss Bingley and Mrs Hurst made very little effort to entertain their guests. Instead, they expected their guests to entertain them. Jane and Elizabeth introduced a number of different topics of conversation, but Miss Bingley had a cutting remark to make about every one of them, while Mrs Hurst spent most of the time yawning behind her hand.

Georgiana and Kitty finished looking at their fashion plates and Georgiana went over to the pianoforte. Kitty did not play, and so Georgiana invited Elizabeth to play a duet with her. Elizabeth agreed readily.

Georgiana was a much better player than Elizabeth. She had had the best masters and she had been made to practise, watched over by various governesses and companions. Elizabeth, on the other hand, had not had any good instruction and she had been left to practise if she wished, but she had never been made to do it. Both young ladies enjoyed it nonetheless. They had a natural affinity, which served them well and enabled them to keep their playing together remarkably well.

Miss Bingley walked over to the pianoforte to listen. Elizabeth was not a proficient, and she did not like the way Miss Bingley smiled every time she played a wrong note, but she knew that Miss Bingley wanted to intimidate her and she refused to be cowed. So she kept on playing, bringing true musicality to the piece, despite some wrong notes.

When Elizabeth looked up at the end of the piece, she caught sight of the mirror on the far wall and saw that the gentlemen had returned from their dinner engagement. Mr Darcy was watching her with a heart-wrenching expression on his face. It was wistful and full of longing, and it set her heart beating more quickly in her chest.

She blushed and turned away from the mirror. She did not turn round until she had gathered her thoughts and her emotions. A few weeks ago, she would have said that Mr Darcy was the most proud and disagreeable man in the world, but now she found him growing on her every day. He had overcome the bad first impression he had made on her and he had replaced it with feelings of admiration, respect, friendship and trust. But it was more than this, much more. She was falling in love with him.

But it would not do to show it. He liked her, she knew. He admired and respected her. But what further feelings did he have for her and how deep did his feelings run?

'How was your evening?' said Miss Bingley, going over to Mr Darcy. 'I hope you had a pleasant time with the officers.'

'Yes, thank you, very pleasant.'

Elizabeth caught sight of Mr Darcy's expression as he said it, and she knew instantly that something was wrong. He looked worried, and there was a crease between his brows. But Mr Darcy, seeing her concern, gave a slight shake of his head. She understood him instantly. He had something to tell her, but he could not speak of it at the moment, most probably because he did not wish Miss Bingley to hear.

The ladies and gentlemen exchanged news of their evenings. Miss Bingley monopolised Mr Darcy until Georgiana invited her to play a duet. The two ladies went over to the pianoforte and began to play.

Mr Bingley fell into conversation with Jane, and Mrs Hurst advised Kitty on a new way to wear her hair, saying condescendingly, 'It would make you look quite pretty.'

Mr Hurst flopped into a chair and fell asleep.

Elizabeth went over to one of the bookshelves at the far end of the room and selected a book. It was well away from the pianoforte, and before long, Mr Darcy followed her.

Elizabeth said, in a low voice. 'Something is wrong. I can tell by your manner. What is it?'

'I have had a shock,' he said. 'We cannot talk of it now, but I would very much appreciate a chance to talk to you about it in the morning.'

'Very well,' she said. 'What is it?'

Mr Darcy said, 'Wickham is here.'

Elizabeth's eyes flew wide in astonishment.

'How do you know?' she asked. 'And what

do you mean by here?'

'I mean here in Meryton. We were dining with the officers, as you know, and one of them mentioned that a friend of Denny's, a Mr George Wickham, had just arrived. He is thinking of joining the militia.'

The militia were stationed in Meryton, and their red coats sent Lydia into a frenzy.

But if Mr Wickham were to join them it would be serious, for it would mean he was intending to stay in the neighbourhood.

Mr Darcy glanced at his sister and his face was full of brotherly concern.

'I must take her back to Pemberley tomorrow, before she has time to hear about it; or, even worse, to meet him. That would be disastrous.'

'I am not so sure,' said Elizabeth thoughtfully.

'What do you mean?' he asked. Then, lowering his voice, he said, 'Wickham has made her terribly unhappy. She has only just started to get over the shock of it all. If she sees him again, it will reopen old wounds and make her miserable all over again.'

'You cannot protect her from meeting him for ever. She is bound to run into him sooner or later, and if she runs into him when she is alone she will be very unhappy and frightened. But if the meeting takes place here, where she is surrounded by family and friends, then she will have the courage to face it. I think it might actually help her to lay her demons to rest.'

Mr Darcy was thoughtful.

'Fears must be faced if they are to be overcome,' said Elizabeth.

'That is true,' he said. 'Even so, I do not wish to distress her. It is difficult to know what to do for the best.'

'Then why not let Georgiana decide?'

He looked over to his sister again. She was looking much brighter and happier than she had done a few short weeks ago. Elizabeth and Kitty's friendship had banished the shadows that had clouded her life since the incident in Ramsgate.

'She is too young to decide,' said Mr Darcy.

'She is not so very young,' said Elizabeth.

'And even telling her will be enough to upset her.'

'To begin with, yes, but once her initial shock is overcome then she will be able to draw strength from her friends and decide whether she feels strong enough to face him. If not, you can take her back to Pemberley.'

'Will you talk to her about it also? She looks to you in a way she cannot look to me. She sees me as an older brother, almost a father, and she does not always find it easy to tell me what she is thinking and feeling. But she sees you as a friend and I know she will confide in you.'

'Yes, I will be happy to help,' said Elizabeth.

She looked over towards Georgiana and thought how difficult it would be for that sweet young lady to meet George Wickham again. But it was better to face the problem than run from it, and once the meeting was over, Georgiana would take strength from the fact that she had done it.

'Then we will call on you tomorrow,' said Mr Darcy, 'for it will be impossible to have a private conversation here.'

There was time for no more. The music, which had been so helpful in disguising their conversation, was drawing to a close.

Mr Darcy walked over to the pianoforte, and when the duet was over, he, Miss Bingley and Georgiana joined the others on the sofas.

A light supper was served, after which it was time for the Miss Bennets to depart.

Mr Darcy and Mr Bingley saw them to the carriage, and Elizabeth felt a warmth spreading through her as Mr Darcy handed her in. Her eyes went instinctively to his and he smiled in a way that set her heart racing. There was something in his glance which told Elizabeth, more eloquently than words, what he felt for her, and that feeling went straight to her heart.

Jane, too, was glowing, as Mr Bingley handed her in beside Elizabeth. Then he kindly handed Kitty in as well.

Elizabeth and Jane were quiet on the way back home, as they both had much to think about, but Kitty was lively, and her chatter made up for their silence.

When they returned to Longbourn, Mrs Bennet wanted to know exactly what they had done all evening, and she would not be content until they had recounted every detail. She wanted to know exactly what Mr Bingley had said to Jane, and exactly what Jane had said in return. She wanted to know if Mr Darcy had paid Elizabeth any attention, and she wanted to make sure that Kitty was getting on well with Georgiana.

'What a useful friend to have!' she said to Kitty. 'When Miss Darcy comes out, she might invite you to some of her balls and you will have a chance to meet a handsome young man with four or five thousand a year!'

Lydia and Mary, fortunately, had gone to bed, so the older girls did not have to put up with Mary's morose comments and Lydia's sighs and complaints.

When Elizabeth and Jane finally retired to their room, they spoke of the evening in quite a different way. They did not have to remember every detail, as they had for their eager mama. They could instead talk about the things that mattered.

Jane confessed that she liked Mr Bingley more and more each time she saw him, and that she was falling in love with him.

Elizabeth confessed that she was falling in

love with Mr Darcy, too.

'Oh, Lizzy, I never knew I could be so happy!' said Jane, her eyes shining.

'Nor did I,' said Elizabeth.

'I wonder when we will see them again?' mused Jane, unpinning her hair and letting it cascade down her back, for she had told the maid that she and Elizabeth could manage on their own.

'Tomorrow,' said Elizabeth.

Then she told Jane all about Mr Wickham, and Jane was happy to offer her assistance in making Georgiana feel comfortable.

'I wonder if Mr Bingley will come with the Darcys when they call tomorrow?' asked Jane dreamily, as she sat down at her dressing table and brushed her long golden hair.

'I am sure he will,' said Elizabeth, climbing into bed. 'How could he resist another chance to see you?'

'Oh! Fie! Lizzy,' said Jane blushing. But she was smiling.

Elizabeth thought it would not be long before Mr Bingley made her sister the happiest of women.

As for Mr Darcy ...

She felt a sudden touch of fear. She knew he liked her. She knew he felt much more than liking for her. His glance had showed her that he was falling in love with her. But would he ever propose? He was a proud man from a great family. Would he be prepared to overthrow the habits of a lifetime and marry someone who was not from his own level in life? She climbed into bed and wished her sister a good night, but she lay awake as Jane blew out the candle. And when she finally fell asleep, Mr Darcy haunted her dreams.

Chapter Ten

Mr Darcy woke early the following morning. He dressed quickly and went out for a ride before eating a hearty breakfast of steak and eggs. He would need all his energy if he was to help his sister.

But it was not his sister he was thinking of, as he finished his breakfast. It was Elizabeth. He had watched her go the previous evening with real regret. He had come to like her, admire her and respect her. But more than that, he knew himself to be in love with her.

He recalled some of Caroline Bingley's earlier teasings. When he had happened to mention Elizabeth's fine eyes, his remarks had fuelled Caroline's jealousy.

"When am I to wish you happy?" she had asked, and he had shaken his head at the ridiculous notion.

But now he did not find it ridiculous. His months in Meryton had shown him that Elizabeth had all the qualities he wanted in a wife, even though he had not known what he wanted before he met her. She had honesty and integrity and compassion. She had loyalty and discretion. She had the kind of beauty that was not immediately apparent, but which became more apparent with every passing day, and she had the loveliest eyes he had ever seen. And, over all these qualities, she had a lively mind and a light-hearted nature which complemented his own serious nature and made her a pleasure to be with. But there was more to it than that. Much more. His feelings for her did not just touch his mind, they touched his soul. They went deeper than anything he had ever known before and he knew they could be only one thing. Love. Her position was not as high as his own, but there were other things in life, more important things, than social standing, and it had taken Elizabeth to show him that.

Once he had resolved the problem of George Wickham, he meant to propose to her. He did not take her acceptance for granted, as once he would have done, before she had taught him that she was not impressed by his wealth and his estate. But, if he was lucky, then she would say yes.

He heard Georgiana's light tread on the stair and so he prepared himself to tell her about George Wickham's arrival in the neighbourhood. And he prepared himself to ask her if she would face him, or if she wanted to return to Pemberley.

Elizabeth looked out of the window as she heard the wheels of a carriage crunching on the gravel below. Sure enough, the Darcy carriage was rolling to a halt in front of the house. Mr Darcy,

Mr Bingley and Miss Darcy climbed out.

Elizabeth went downstairs, smoothing the skirt of her spotted muslin gown as she did so. She patted her hair in place, and glanced in one of the mirrors in the hall to make sure she was tidy before she went into the drawing-room to greet her guests.

'Mr Bingley! Mr Darcy! Miss Darcy!' said Mrs Bennet, throwing her arms wide to welcome them. 'How good it is to see you again!'

Mrs Bennet continued to embarrass everyone with her effusions until at last, mercifully, she rang for refreshments and the act of drinking tea prohibited any further loud displays of delight.

Elizabeth wondered how she was going to find some time alone with Georgiana, who looked pale, but luckily the problem was solved for her. Mrs Bennet, with a wink at Mary and a surreptitious kick to Lydia's foot, succeeded in drawing her two youngest daughters out of the room. Kitty, fortunately, was late rising, as she was tired from the night before, so that only Mr Bingley and Jane, Mr Darcy, Miss Darcy and Elizabeth remained.

Elizabeth glanced at Mr Bingley and looked enquiringly at Mr Darcy, but a swift shake of Mr Darcy's head showed her that Mr Bingley did not know everything. So she refrained from speaking until Jane had taken Mr Bingley over to the other end of the room in order to show him some of her watercolours.

'My brother has told me everything,' said Georgiana to Elizabeth. 'I am so pleased he has given me a choice of whether to go or whether to stay.'

'And which do you choose?' asked Elizabeth.

'I choose to stay,' said Georgiana, with a lift of her chin.

'Bravo!' said Elizabeth. 'When next you meet Mr Wickham, it will be with friends and family around you. In fact, I suggest we go now. Mama was talking about Mr Wickham this morning over breakfast and saying that he likes to walk up and down the high street in the mornings – there is not much news in a small town and so everything our new arrival does is talked about,' Elizabeth explained. 'We will all go, all five of us. Do not worry, Georgiana. You will not be the one feeling uncomfortable. It will be Mr Wickham who is feeling uncomfortable and unhappy by the end of the morning.'

'I believe it will,' said Georgiana, sounding more cheerful.

'There is no time like the present,' said Elizabeth, rising.

She suggested the idea of a walk to Jane, who agreed at once, and Mr Bingley said the idea was charming.

Mrs Bennet entered the room at that moment, and who could tell if it was a lucky chance or if that indefatigable woman had been listening at the keyhole? But she could not have heard any of the confidences, as they had been spoken in a low voice, and could only have heard of the plan to walk into Meryton.

'The very thing!' she said.

She gave Elizabeth some commissions and before very long the party set out.

Elizabeth walked on one side of Georgiana, and Mr Darcy walked on the other side.

Jane and Mr Bingley walked behind her, and all of them gave her strength and courage by their presence.

The day was fine, although there was an autumnal nip in the air, and so they walked briskly. The trees that lined the country lane waved bare branches in the wind, and the fallen leaves swished beneath the party's feet.

Soon they approached the town. The fields gave way to cobbled streets, and shops began to appear on either side of them. There was noise and bustle as people went about their daily tasks, and the scene was a lively one.

They made their way to the circulating library, and they had almost reached it when, round the corner, came Mr Wickham with one of the officers, Mr Denny.

'Courage!' said Elizabeth softly to Georgiana.

Georgiana reached for Elizabeth's hand and gave it a squeeze.

Elizabeth squeezed it back, giving her strength, and she felt Georgiana stand tall beside her.

Mr Wickham, on the other hand, seemed to shrink. His charming smirk, which had covered his face as they met, grew more hesitant. And it was small wonder. The cool disdain coming from Elizabeth's party was enough to make any man lose his confidence.

As Mr Wickham's confidence shrank, so Georgiana's confidence grew.

'Mr Wickham,' said Georgiana. 'What a surprise. I did not expect to see you here.'

'Nor I,' said Mr Darcy, in his most arrogant voice. 'Are you staying in the neighbourhood?'

'I am sure Mr Wickham is just passing through. There is very little for a man of his type here,' said Elizabeth, with steel beneath her polite veneer. 'I have lived in Meryton all my life and I doubt if he will find it to his tastes. I am sure he will be happier elsewhere.'

Mr Denny sensed something of the hostility in the air and said doubtfully, 'Oh, I don't know, it's not a bad place. Wickham is thinking of joining the militia, which will keep him here.'

'Indeed?' said Elizabeth, raising her eyebrows and looking at Mr Wickham pointedly.

Mr Wickham squirmed, but he kept the smile on his face.

'I have not decided yet,' he said. 'I was considering joining the militia, it is true, but I am not sure the air here agrees with me.'

'I think it an excellent idea. You must join the

army,' said Mr Darcy. 'In fact, I would be willing to purchase you a commission. I know of one that has fallen vacant in the Indies.'

'The Indies?' asked Wickham, shocked, for the Indies were practically on the other side of the world.

'The Indies,' said Mr Darcy firmly.

'Indeed, I am sure the air there would suit you very well,' said Elizabeth.

Mr Wickham glanced at Jane, who remarked, 'Oh, yes, the Indies. What an excellent idea.'

'I will send my man of business to you,' said Mr Darcy. 'You can be out of the country by the end of the week.'

'I really don't know —' began Mr Wickham.

'I do,' said Mr Darcy.

'And I,' said Elizabeth.

'And I,' said Georgiana.

'The sooner the better,' said Elizabeth. 'You look rather pale to me, Mr Wickham, you need some sunshine. I am sure you will be very unhappy if you stay here.'

Mr Denny, who had not been able to follow the conversation, seized on the only part of the conversation he had understood.

'A commission, Wickham! What a generous offer. This is the chance of a lifetime! You are fortunate indeed.'

'Damn you, Darcy!' broke out Mr Wickham.

Mr Denny looked at him in astonishment, but Mr Darcy was unperturbed.

Mr Wickham turned on his heel and walked off.

'What was all that about?' asked Mr Denny in surprise.

'I believe Mr Wickham must have been hoping for a commission elsewhere,' said Mr Darcy smoothly.

'Ungrateful wretch. But he'll soon see sense. He has pockets to let and cannot afford to turn this chance down. It's decent of you, Darcy. Jolly decent,' said Mr Denny.

Mr Darcy bowed, there were a few more polite comments, and then Mr Denny went on his way.

Elizabeth laughed, and Georgiana joined in with her laughter.

Mr Bingley looked baffled.

'A private joke,' Mr Darcy explained.

'Ah!'

Mr Bingley did not understand, but he was not of an enquiring disposition and so he was satisfied.

They purchased the items Mrs Bennet had asked for and then returned to Longbourn.

Mrs Bennet was eager to hear all the news, and Mr Bingley delighted her beyond her wildest dreams by saying that he had been thinking of holding a ball at Netherfield Park.

Lydia jumped up from the sofa in great excitement, and even Mary was heard to say that she might be persuaded to take a rest from her studies and join the party.

Elizabeth parted from Georgiana with real affection, and was very pleased to see that Georgiana's eyes were bright.

Mr Darcy's happiness was also easy to see.

'That was an inspired offer,' said Elizabeth to him merrily as they parted.

'I don't know why I didn't think of it sooner,' he returned. 'It came to me as we stood there talking. It will not only spare Georgiana the possibility of bumping into Mr Wickham, it will spare me that possibility, too. And it has shown that George and I have parted as friends – or, at least, that is the way it will appear to the outside world - so that if ever he decides to try and spread any rumours of a rift between us, no one will believe him.'

Elizabeth smiled.

His own expression warmed.

'Thank you for everything you have done for Georgiana – and for me. I wonder, would you do me the honour of accepting my hand for the first dance at the Netherfield Ball?'

Elizabeth blushed.

'I would be delighted,' she said.

Chapter Eleven

Mrs Bennet was cast into a frenzy by the thought of the Netherfield ball. She spent many hours looking through Jane and Elizabeth's wardrobes to make sure they would both have something lovely to wear.

'What a pity there is not enough time to have a new dress made for each of you, but your white muslins are almost new and they look very well. You must have new gloves and new fans. I insist upon it.'

Mr Bennet was forced to agree, for otherwise Mrs Bennet would not have given him any peace.

There was a spell of wet weather which made it impossible for the Miss Bennets to walk into Meryton, but the servants went, and returned with two new pairs of long white evening gloves, as well as new painted fans. They also bought some white lace, which Jane and Elizabeth used to trim the sleeves and hems of their gowns.

At last, everything was ready. Jane and Elizabeth spent the afternoon preparing, bathing and washing their hair, which the maid arranged into a fashionable bun for each other them, sweeping their hair off their faces and pinning it high at the back of their heads.

They complemented each other perfectly. Jane was a radiant blonde, with glowing golden hair, while Elizabeth was a lovely brunette, with shining dark brown tresses.

Lydia, Kitty and Mary were also to join in the fun. Mrs Bennet had made some effort with their clothes, too, though not as much as she had with Jane and Elizabeth. She was very gratified that her daughters had found such refined friends, and she hoped that her younger girls might meet some eligible gentlemen at the ball.

At last they set off. The moon was full and it brightened the way to Netherfield Park. The imposing residence looked magical in the moonlight. Carriages were rolling up in front of the door, with snorting horses and skilful coachman all adding to the excitement of the scene. Light flooded out of the windows and pooled on the steps, which were crowded with people.

Elizabeth lifted the hem of her skirt as she followed Jane out of the carriage. They went across the gravel drive and up the stone steps. Once inside, they crossed the black-and-white floor, threading their way between the marble columns. There were gentleman in blue coats and black, and there were officers in scarlet coats with gold epaulettes. There were young ladies in white muslin and older ladies in brightly coloured gowns. It was a wonderful sight.

The Bennets were shown to a special room

which had been set aside so the ladies could remove their outdoor clothes. Jane and Elizabeth removed their cloaks and bonnets, then sat down together on one of the gilded settees as they took off their outdoor shoes and slipped on their soft white dancing pumps.

Lydia was as noisy as ever, and Mary preached at her, while Mrs Bennet fussed over all of them, but Kitty was remarkably grown up. Elizabeth was pleased to see what a good effect Georgiana was having on her younger sister.

And then it was time to go into the drawing-room.

Elizabeth looked around the room with a fluttering heart, and when she saw Mr Darcy looking very noble and handsome at the far side of the room, in his black coat and white breeches, she flushed with pleasure. His white shirt was frilled at the cuffs and down the front, and his cravat was fastened with a diamond tie pin. His dark hair was arranged in a fashionable style which set off his eyes, his cheekbones and the firm line of his jaw.

As soon as he saw her, his whole countenance changed and he walked towards her with an eager step and claimed her for the first dance.

They took their place in the set, standing opposite each other. Mr Darcy bowed and Elizabeth dropped an elegant curtsey, with her back straight and her gown sweeping beneath her.

Then the dance began. They danced without speaking, not because they did not have anything to say to each other, but because they were both too happy to speak. Their eyes said everything that needed to be said.

Elizabeth was lost in a haze of happiness and her feet hardly seemed to touch the ground. It was as if Mr Darcy was the only other person in the room. She felt she belonged with him and had always belonged with him and always would belong with him, for all eternity.

When the dance ended, Mr Darcy gave her his arm and led her into the refreshment room. Tall windows looked out over the terrace and, further down, one of them was open despite the lateness of the year. It looked so beautiful, with the moon and starlight silvering the terrace and the gardens beyond, that without thinking about it they both stepped outside.

Elizabeth gave an involuntary shiver and Mr Darcy took off his coat and put it round her shoulders. She accepted it gracefully.

'Elizabeth . . . ' He sank to one knee, there in the moonlight. 'I can wait no longer. I have felt my love for you growing ever since I came to Netherfield. It has been deepening and strengthening every day, until I can no longer contain it. I belong to you, Elizabeth, body and soul. You would make me the happiest of men if you would agree to become my wife.' He took her hand. 'Will you, Lizzy? Will you marry me.'

She looked down at him with radiant eyes and a heart full of love and said, 'Yes.'

The word came out as a whisper, so emotional did she feel, but it did not matter. He heard her and that was all that was needed. He stood up and took her in his arms and her face turned instinctively up to his and he kissed her. Nothing else seemed to exist, only the two of them and their love for each other.

At last the kiss ended and they smiled at each other, shyly at first and then happily.

'I must ask your father for his permission,' said Mr Darcy. 'I will speak to him tomorrow, when he is at liberty. I will have to share you with other people then. But for now, I want you to myself.'

Elizabeth felt the same. It was too precious a moment to be shared with anyone else. She looked around her, at the moonlit night and the silvered grounds of Netherfield Park and the house alight with candles, and then again at Mr Darcy, and she knew it was something she would remember for the rest of her life.

Chapter Twelve

Mr Darcy dressed carefully the following morning. He wanted to make a good impression on Mr Bennet when he asked for Elizabeth's hand in marriage. The two men had often talked, for they had met at various entertainments, and although they saw each other's faults, they had a liking for each other. Mr Darcy was prepared to answer Mr Bennet's questions in order to reassure him that Elizabeth would be happy.

Having finished tying his cravat, Mr Darcy put on his tailcoat, flicked a speck of fluff from his breeches and went downstairs. He found Mr Bingley already there. Mr Bingley was sitting in front of a plate of ham and eggs but he was not eating. He looked very nervous.

'I say, Darcy,' said Mr Bingley, as Mr Darcy helped himself to a steak.

'Yes?' said Mr Darcy, sitting down opposite his friend.

'I really do like Miss Bennet very much. In fact, I don't just like her . . . ' He seemed to gather his courage and finished in a rush, ' . . . I love her. I know you think marriages should be between people of equal rank, but I have decided to ask Miss Bennet to be my wife anyway.'

He looked at Mr Darcy rather guiltily, but

with strength of purpose.

'I think it is an excellent idea!' said Mr Darcy, his face breaking into a smile.

He reached over the table and shook his friend by the hand.

'You do?' asked Mr Bingley in surprise, but nevertheless looking very pleased.

'Yes, I do. My views on marriage have undergone a complete change in the last few months. And anyway, I cannot blame you for proposing to Miss Bennet. You see, last night I asked Miss Elizabeth to be my wife.'

Mr Bingley looked surprised and then delighted.

'Capital!' he said, with a wide smile. 'She is a lovely young woman. She will be very good for you. She gives you just the lightness you need and you give her . . . well, you will give her Pemberley!' he finished, joking.

Mr Darcy laughed. 'Yes, Bingley, I will. But I will give her more than that, and she, of all the women I have ever met, knows it. She is unique. She is the only woman I have ever met who was able to pierce my pride and show me what it was like to be valued for myself. She had the courage to stand up to me and tell me when I was wrong, and she had the goodness and the justice to forgive me my errors and reward me with her hand in marriage. She has made me the happiest of men.'

'Oh, no,' said Mr Bingley, shaking his head

with a smile. 'That honour belongs to me!'

'We will have to agree to differ on that. I am going to see Mr Bennet as soon as I have eaten.'

'And I will be doing the same,' said Mr Bingley.

'Mr Bennet will be very busy this morning, then!' said Mr Darcy. 'As you have not asked Miss Bennet yet, I will speak to him first and you can follow.'

'Agreed,' said Mr Bingley. 'But, if you are not unwilling, we can go in the carriage together.'

Mr Darcy nodded.

The two gentlemen tried to finish their breakfast but they were too nervous to eat and before very long they set out for Longbourn.

Elizabeth woke late that morning. The ball had gone on until the early hours and when she had returned home she had been too excited and happy to sleep. So it was almost ten o'clock when she awoke. She looked over to her sister's bed and saw that Jane, too, was only just waking.

They smiled at each other and began to rise in a leisurely fashion. But the door was flung open and Mrs Bennet rushed in.

'Lizzy! Jane! Make haste. Oh, Hill, help them. Where is your corset, Lizzy? Oh, Jane, where is your sash?'

'What is it?' asked Elizabeth. 'Is the house on fire?'

'House on fire! House on fire! It is something far more important than that! Elizabeth, Mr Darcy is in your father's study and he wants to marry you!'

Elizabeth laughed for joy.

'And Mr Bingley is in the drawing-room, Jane. If you are clever he will ask you to marry him, ' said Mrs Bennet.

'Jane does not need to be clever – although, of course, she is,' said Elizabeth. 'Mr Bingley has already fallen in love with her and I am convinced she will soon be Mrs Bingley.'

Mrs Bennet collapsed on the bed, stupefied by so much good news.

But she quickly rallied.

'They are bound to have brothers and cousins and friends. Make sure they bring them all to Longbourn! Your sisters still need husbands,' said Mrs Bennet.

She was at last persuaded to leave the room.

Elizabeth and Jane dressed quickly. Hill brought them some hot chocolate to drink and some warm rolls to eat and then they went downstairs. Jane went into the drawing-room to be with Mr Bingley and Elizabeth lingered in the hall, for she heard Mr Darcy's voice and knew he was just about to leave the study.

The door opened and Mr Darcy came out. She could see by his face that her father had given his consent.

He took her hands and kissed her, then they

went into the drawing-room. Mr Bingley slipped out of the door, to take his turn in speaking to Mr Bennet.

Mrs Bennet was loud in her congratulations.

Jane, seeing Lizzy's embarrassment, took her mother out into the garden on some pretext and Elizabeth was left alone with Mr Darcy.

'I have your father's permission, and so now nothing can prevent our marriage,' said Mr Darcy. He turned to face her. 'I cannot believe I was lucky enough to find you. You didn't just rescue Georgiana, all those months ago in Ramsgate, you rescued me. You rescued me from the cold, distant world I had built around myself and brought me into a world of light and warmth. You awakened feelings I thought I had lost for ever. You saved me from loneliness and unhappiness, Lizzy, and taught me to love.'

Mrs Bennet's voice drifted in through the window.

' . . . . ten thousand a year!'

'And now I can save you!' he said with a smile.

Elizabeth laughed. It would certainly be pleasant to be saved from her mother! But she was not marrying to escape from her mother. She was marrying because she had found the one man in all the world she loved.

And to make matters even better, her beloved Jane had found the man she loved, too.

Through the window she saw Mr Bingley

approaching Jane. He had been to see Mr Bennet, and from his happy face it was obvious he had been given permission to marry Jane.

'Who would have thought, when I accepted my aunt's invitation to go to Ramsgate, that so much would happen?' asked Elizabeth. 'Or that, after such a bad start, everything would turn out so well?'

'And now we have nothing more to do except enjoy our lives together,' said Mr Darcy.

Printed in Dunstable, United Kingdom